TELL ME WHAT'S WRONG.

The phone rang. Stevie leaned over to grab the receiver. "Hello?" she said cheerfully.

"Stevie? Is that you?"

"Phil?" she said with a little frown, barely recognizing his voice. She hadn't spoken to him since she'd seen him on Tuesday afternoon. "What's wrong?"

"I need to see you." His words sounded so strangled with worry that Stevie's heart immediately started beating faster with concern. "Can you meet me somewhere? Right away?"

"Sure," Stevie replied, her hand gripping the receiver tightly. "But what is it? What happened?"

"I don't—Just meet me at that spot at the picnic grounds as soon as you can, okay?"

**Don't miss any of the excitement
at PINE HOLLOW,
where friends come first:**

And coming in August 1999:

PINE HOLLOW™

SHYING AT TROUBLE

BY BONNIE BRYANT

BANTAM BOOKS
NEW YORK • TORONTO • LONDON • SYDNEY • AUCKLAND

Special thanks to Sir "B" Farms and Laura and Vinny Marino

RL 5.0, ages 12 and up

SHYING AT TROUBLE
A Bantam Book / June 1999

"Pine Hollow" is a trademark of Bonnie Bryant Hiller.

ISBN 0-553-49247-0

Published simultaneously in the United States and Canada.

Bantam Books are published by Bantam Books, a division of Random
House, Inc. Its trademark, consisting of the words "Bantam Books" and
the portrayal of a rooster, is Registered in U.S. Patent and Trademark
Office and in other countries. Marca Registrada. Bantam Books, 1540
Broadway, New York, New York 10036.

PRINTED IN THE UNITED STATES OF AMERICA

OPM   0 9 8 7 6 5 4 3 2 1

My special thanks to Catherine Hapka for her help in the writing of this book.

ONE

"Lisa! Honey, I'm home!"

Lisa Atwood looked up from her history essay and blinked in surprise. "Mom?" she called back uncertainly. She'd been concentrating so hard on her paper that she hadn't even heard her mother's car pull up. She stood, stretched, and headed out of her room and down the hall.

Her eyes confirmed what her ears had told her—her mother was in a good mood for a change. Mrs. Atwood was bustling about near the door, setting down a pair of large shopping bags, shrugging off her light autumn jacket, and brushing her chin-length, graying brown hair out of her eyes.

When she saw Lisa coming downstairs, Mrs. Atwood's smile grew wider. "There you are, sweetie!" she cried, clapping her hands gleefully. "I was hoping you'd be home. I have a surprise for you."

"A surprise?" Lisa glanced warily at the bulging

1

shopping bags, both of which bore the name of the clothing store at the Willow Creek Mall where her mother worked as an assistant manager. If anything could have ruined Mrs. Atwood's life-long love of shopping, it would have been working at that store. The manager was a smarmy slob who often expected Mrs. Atwood and the other assistant manager to make up for his laziness and stupid mistakes. The other employees were generally high-school or college students, and they didn't usually last long enough for Mrs. Atwood to get to know them even if she'd wanted to. None of that had seemed so bad back when Mrs. Atwood had started working at the store part-time for a little extra spending money. But since she and Mr. Atwood had divorced, things had changed. Suddenly the stories didn't seem so amusing anymore, and her tone when she described her boss's latest outrages no longer held any trace of amusement or irony.

Mrs. Atwood didn't notice Lisa's thoughtful expression. She was too busy digging through the larger of the two shopping bags. Lisa did her best to hold back a sigh as she watched. Somehow, her mother's happy expression made her feel sad and wistful. It reminded her of how her mother used to be before Lisa's father left, shattering his wife's entire world. Mrs. Atwood had never exactly been a bundle of fun, but she had been satisfied with her life and her family. Lisa hadn't had to worry about her back then. She hadn't had to do most of the cooking and cleaning, either, or fill in as her mother's only reliable friend and confidante.

Mrs. Atwood stood up, clutching a bundle of shimmery midnight blue fabric. "Surprise!" she cried cheerily. She shook out the fabric with a flourish, and Lisa could see that it was a dress—a sleek, stylish dress with a high neckline and cap sleeves. "It's a brand-new style we're carrying this fall. The shipment came in yesterday, but I didn't get around to opening the box until today, and as soon as I did I thought of you. It's perfect for someone with your slim figure and your coloring. Do you love it?"

Lisa did her best to smile and look excited, playing along. "It's gorgeous, Mom," she said, reaching out to rub her fingers over the smooth fabric, wincing a little as she noticed the hefty figure on the price tag dangling from one sleeve. Even with her employee discount, the dress had still cost Mrs. Atwood more than she could afford, especially for something so unnecessary. "It's great. Um, I think it's a little too dressy for school, though."

Mrs. Atwood laughed. "Don't be silly, dear," she said. "An outfit this special isn't for school. I thought you could wear it the next time you go to a party or a dance or out on a special date with

Alex. You don't have many dressy outfits, and you're at that age when you're going to want to start dressing up more."

Lisa didn't bother to tell her mother that her feelings about clothes hadn't changed, no matter what age she was. Now seventeen, she still felt every bit as comfortable in neat but casual clothes—like the khakis and cotton sweater she was wearing that day—as she had at seven, or fourteen, or sixteen and a half. Her classic outfits complemented her classic looks—her straight, shiny blond hair; her large, expressive eyes fringed by long lashes; her slender figure. She wasn't sure the new outfit was really her. It was a little flashy, a little trendy for her taste. But she didn't intend to tell her mother that—not when she was so excited about her surprise.

Surprises, Lisa thought ruefully as she took the dress and smoothed it carefully over her arm. She noticed that her mother was bending over the second shopping bag. She couldn't help grimacing a little, fully expecting a pair of midnight blue pumps to come out of the bag to match her new dress. *Surprises are supposed to be fun and exciting, but they never turn out quite the way they should, do they? Especially these days.*

As surprises went, the gift of an inappropriate outfit was hardly the most unsettling one Lisa had had to deal with lately. Lisa had never liked surprises much—she was a logical, cautious person, a planner, and she liked to know what was coming so that she could prepare herself. That was one reason she had been so thrown by the news she'd learned the week before about Prancer, a horse at the stable where she rode. Lisa had ridden Prancer almost exclusively for years—almost since the elegant Thoroughbred mare had first retired from the racetrack and come to Pine Hollow Stables.

That had changed a little over a month ago, soon after Lisa had returned from spending the summer in California with her father. Max Regnery, the owner of Pine Hollow, had suddenly declared Prancer off-limits without explaining why. Lisa had wondered and worried about the mare for weeks before finally, accidentally, finding out the truth: Prancer was pregnant with twins, an unusual and sometimes risky situation for a horse. As if that surprise hadn't been bad enough, Max's revelation had been accompanied by the even more surprising fact that one of Lisa's best friends had known about it all along.

Lisa had met Carole Hanson and Stevie Lake on her first day at Pine Hollow some four years earlier. The three girls had bonded almost immediately over their love of horses and riding, even forming a club they had named The Saddle Club to give themselves an excuse to talk about their favorite activity even more.

But the one thing that had always been even more important than horses to the girls was their friendship. That friendship had sometimes seemed surprising to outsiders, since the three of them were so very different in so many ways. In contrast to Lisa's mature, steady, responsible personality, Stevie was always fun-loving, freewheeling, and a bit of a daredevil. Sometimes Lisa thought that the only thing steady about Stevie was her relationship with her longtime boyfriend, Phil Marsten. The two had been completely committed to each other since meeting at riding camp years earlier, despite the fact that they lived in neighboring towns and attended different schools.

And then there was Carole. From the beginning, the girls had all agreed that Carole was the horse-craziest of the three of them. She boarded her horse, an eager, friendly, big bay named Starlight, at Pine Hollow, and her friends liked to joke that she spent more time at the stable than he did. That wasn't far from the truth. Carole planned to spend her life working around horses, and she had started by taking on an after-school job at Pine Hollow, where she had quickly become an invaluable part of Max's small staff. She never seemed to miss a step at the stable, even when she was busy with four or five different tasks at once, but she could be quite scatterbrained in the outside world, often forgetting the most basic things in a way that made super-organized Lisa squirm with frustration.

Still, despite all their differences, the three girls had always been a tight-knit trio. Even now that they were all in high school and had a lot of new distractions and responsibilities, they spent a lot of their free time together. Until a few days earlier, Lisa could never have imagined that Carole could ever do anything to jeopardize their three-way friendship.

Even now that she'd had a few days to get used to the idea, Lisa could hardly believe that Carole hadn't told her the truth about Prancer. Carole must have realized Lisa was driving herself crazy with worry, and that she could be trusted to keep a confidence. But Carole hadn't said a word about Prancer's condition, the real reason for Max's ban on riding the mare. She'd let her friend wait and worry and wonder until finally someone else had told her.

For the first couple of days, Lisa had been absolutely livid. But the more time passed, the more her anger shifted to regret and sadness. She wished there was a way they could all go back in time and try again. That way, Carole might decide to tell her the truth about Prancer and this whole stupid fight would never have happened. . . .

But Lisa was practical enough not to waste much time on that sort of wishful thinking. She just wished she knew how to proceed—how to find a way to forgive Carole completely and get their friendship back on track. *If that's what Carole wants, that is,* she added.

Lisa sighed and forced herself to return her attention to her mother, who was busy unveiling a large tissue-wrapped item she had pulled out of her second bag. That self-satisfied little smile was still on her face as she glanced at Lisa with an almost mischievous gleam in her brown eyes. "But that's not all," she said. "Since you were getting a new outfit, I thought I ought to have one, too. Fair's fair, right?" She held up another dress. This one was in her own size, pearl gray with shell buttons.

Lisa blinked. She couldn't see the price tag on her mother's new dress, but she suspected it was just as expensive as her own. While shopping had remained one of Mrs. Atwood's favorite pastimes even after the divorce, she rarely indulged anymore in this kind of impulse buying. What had brought on this sudden extravagance?

"That'll look great on you, Mom," Lisa said.

"Thanks, sweetie." Mrs. Atwood held the soft gray dress against herself and preened self-consciously in the hallway mirror, brushing her hair off her forehead and pursing her lips appraisingly at her own reflection.

As she watched, Lisa decided that maybe she

shouldn't spend so much time analyzing her mother's behavior. She should just be thankful that she seemed happier than she had in ages and let it go at that.

After all, Mom deserves a little indulgence once in a while, she thought, studying the lines around her mother's eyes and mouth, the result of too many grim and lonely days and nights since Mr. Atwood had moved out. *She's been working extra hard lately. As if her regular hours aren't tough enough, now that jerk has her doing inventory until the middle of the night, too.* Lisa shook her head and frowned slightly at the thought. The night before, Lisa's mother hadn't gotten home until almost midnight, even though the mall closed at nine-thirty. *When she spends her Saturday night like that, it's no wonder she needs a little cheering up now and then. Right?*

She bit her lip. *Besides, it's not like I don't have enough problems of my own right now,* she thought a little defensively. Not only was there the situation with Carole, compounded by Lisa's almost constant sense of worry about Prancer's pregnancy, but most of her other friends seemed to be having troubles of one sort or another. Phil's best friend, A.J., was acting weird, though nobody quite knew why. The only thing they knew was that the fun-loving, friendly A.J. they'd all known had been replaced by a silent, sullen A.J. who spent most of his time brooding in his room. Stevie and Phil had been so worried that they'd started looking for any solution they could find. The day before, they had arranged for all of A.J.'s friends to gather at his house to confront him and try to find out what was going on with him. An intervention, Stevie had called it. Lisa, however, couldn't help thinking of it as more of a confrontation, since they didn't know what was wrong with A.J. or how to help him. All they could hope was that if he realized how many friends he had and how worried about him they were, he would tell them what was wrong. Then they could all try to find a solution together. Lisa and her boyfriend, Alex, had attended the event, but as it turned out, it hadn't done much good. As soon as he'd realized what was happening, A.J. had escaped to his room, locked the door, turned up the stereo, and that had been the end of that.

At the same time, Lisa had found out about another disaster, this time involving a newer friend, Callie Forester. Callie's family had moved to town several months earlier, and the week before, a friend from her old hometown on the West Coast had come for a visit. Upon her return home, the girl had written a gossipy tell-all article for her local newspaper. The article had been picked up by the national press, probably because Callie's father, a congressman, had recently signed on to be the head of a controversial new welfare committee. He and the rest of the family had been terribly embarrassed by the article, but no one had been hurt more than Callie herself. Not only were all her most personal secrets printed in black and white for the entire nation to read, but it had all come about because one of her oldest friends in the world had betrayed her trust.

And then there was Alex. . . .

Suddenly Lisa noticed that her mother had turned away from the mirror and was looking at her. "Darling," Mrs. Atwood said, "why don't you go slip into your new dress? We should make sure it fits."

"All right," Lisa agreed. Playing dress-up was the last thing she felt like doing. She had that history paper to finish and a dozen calculus problems to do. But her mother looked so eager, so happy, and she had so little happiness in her life at the moment. . . . "I'll go put it on right now."

She hurried back up the stairs and down the hall to her bedroom. Tossing the new dress on her neat, rose-patterned bedspread, she automatically started pulling off her sweater. But her mind had already returned to its previous topic.

A few years ago Lisa would have laughed at the idea that Alex Lake would turn out to be her soul mate. Alex had always been around, but it hadn't been until the year before that Lisa had started to notice him as something more than Stevie's smart, athletic, slightly goofy twin brother. All of a sudden she had realized that he was his own unique, special person, and around that same time something in the way he looked at her had hinted that he, too, had begun to see her differently. In the midst of her heartache and confusion over her parents' breakup, her father's remarriage, and the birth of her baby sister, falling in love with Alex had come as a wonderful, refreshing surprise—like stepping out of a stuffy, dark, overheated room into a crisp, breezy autumn morning.

Her relationship with Alex had only grown stronger and deeper since then. That was why she was so troubled by the secret that lay between them now. Lisa had been doing her best to bury this particular concern deep down in the recesses of her mind, not wanting to deal with it when so many other things seemed more pressing. But she couldn't ever quite forget that it was there, waiting, daring her to get too complacent. She knew she had to find a way to tell him soon, before too much more time had passed. If she didn't, she would have to figure out how to live with the knowledge that their relationship, once so completely open and honest and trusting, now held a secret they didn't share. She wasn't sure she could tell him, especially when she thought of how he might react when he heard that she had almost decided to spend her senior year living with her father in California instead of returning home to Willow Creek, to him, but she wasn't sure she had any choice.

She quickly straightened the hem of the blue dress and surveyed herself critically in the full-length mirror on the back of her door. She had to admit that the dress didn't look as strange as she had expected it would. In fact, she looked almost . . . snazzy. Sexy, even. She wondered what Alex would think if he ever saw her in it.

"Not that I have anyplace to wear it," she muttered to her own reflection. She and Alex often attended the dances that were held at Willow Creek High School, where she was a senior, and at Fenton Hall, the private school where he was a junior. While students at both schools tended to dress up a bit more than normal for the dances, a fancy party dress like the one Lisa was wearing would be as out of place as a mule at the Kentucky Derby. "And it's not exactly the kind of thing I'd wear to the stable or the movie theater at the mall."

She grinned as she imagined Max's expression if she turned up to muck out stalls in that getup. *Maybe I should get a matching gold-plated pitchfork,* she thought a bit giddily. *Or a special dressy hard hat with sequins and bows.* She shook her head, amused at her own silly thoughts. Maybe her mother's rare good mood was rubbing off on her.

That reminded her that her mother was waiting downstairs to see her in her new finery. Giving herself one last glance in the mirror, she headed for the door.

"Ta-daaa!" Lisa hurried down the last few steps with her arms spread wide, ready to twirl and pose to her mother's heart's content. But she stopped short, her face turning pink, when she realized that her mother wasn't alone.

"Look, Lisa!" Mrs. Atwood cried cheerily. "Another nice surprise. Carole's here!"

Carole was casting Mrs. Atwood a sidelong glance, looking a bit startled at the woman's high spirits. Lisa was feeling plenty startled herself. She gulped, wondering what Carole was doing there. Had she come to make up, to apologize? Lisa had begun to wonder whether Carole even remembered they were fighting—she had barely cast Lisa a glance the day before when they were all at A.J.'s.

"Hi," Carole said tentatively as Lisa stepped forward. "Um, can we talk?"

"I don't know," Lisa replied warily. "Do we have anything to talk about?"

Mrs. Atwood was sizing Lisa up, beaming contentedly, completely unaware of the tension between the two girls. "Oh, darling!" she exclaimed.

"I was right. That dress is absolutely perfect on you!"

"Thanks, Mom." Lisa forced herself to keep her voice normal. She wished her mother would go away so that she and Carole could say what they really wanted to say, whatever that might be, but she didn't dare suggest it. Mrs. Atwood was so sensitive, and the last thing Lisa wanted to do was ruin her good mood.

Mrs. Atwood reached to adjust the collar of Lisa's dress. "All right then," she said. "You'd better take it off and hang it up before it gets wrinkled. Why don't you two girls run along upstairs and do that? I'm dying for a cup of tea."

"Okay," Lisa said, hardly daring to believe her luck. For once, it seemed, her mother wasn't desperate for her company. That was certainly unusual, but she wasn't about to question it. "See you later, Mom."

"It's lovely to see you as always, Carole," Mrs. Atwood said. "Now you make sure Lisa hangs up that dress right away, okay? Don't get her talking about horses so she forgets."

"I won't," Carole promised with a smile that looked a bit forced.

Mrs. Atwood smiled back. Then she headed toward the kitchen, humming under her breath.

Once the two girls were alone, Carole turned back to Lisa, her large, deep brown eyes serious

15

once again. "I've been thinking," she said earnestly. "I feel terrible that we've been fighting."

Lisa wasn't sure what to say. She felt bad about their fight, too. But she couldn't help remembering how it had started—Carole had kept an important secret from her. "Me too," she said. "But the thing with Prancer—"

"I know," Carole interrupted. "That was mostly my fault, I guess." She shifted her feet nervously and bit her lip. "Things have just been so busy lately, with work and school and Samson's training. . . . I'm not making excuses. I'm just trying to explain. But mostly I'm trying to say that I'm really sorry for what happened."

Her face and voice were so sincere, so completely Carole-like in their trusting hopefulness, that Lisa softened immediately. Suddenly everything she'd been so angry about didn't seem quite as important anymore—not as important as a four-year friendship, anyway. *Maybe Mom's mood really is rubbing off on me,* she thought. "Why don't we go upstairs?" she said to Carole. "If I don't put this dress away, Mom will freak out. Then we can talk."

Carole nodded quickly. "That would be great."

Neither girl said a word as they walked up the stairs together and entered Lisa's room. Pushing the door closed, Lisa headed for her desk and perched on the edge of the chair. Carole seemed slightly uncomfortable. Instead of flopping into the rose-patterned lounge chair as she usually did, she hovered near the door, leaning tentatively against Lisa's dresser.

"Well," Lisa said after another moment of silence. "Um . . ."

"I'm really sorry," Carole said in a rush. "I should have known you'd be worried about Prancer. I should have realized how you'd be feeling."

You should have told me the truth, Lisa thought. But she didn't say it. "Well," she said instead, "I wish Max hadn't asked you not to tell anyone. I really thought Prancer must be horribly sick or dying or something, since no one was talking."

"I know." Carole looked contrite. "That wasn't fair. I know Max wanted to keep this quiet, but sometimes secrets are more trouble than they're worth, you know?"

"I know." Lisa's mind flashed to Alex for a moment. But she pushed the thought aside. "I just wish you'd trusted me. You know I wouldn't have breathed a word to anyone if I knew Max didn't want people to know."

"I know that," Carole said. "I guess maybe I just forgot. Or I was confused, you know? Trying to do the right thing . . . Anyway, I don't blame you for being mad and everything. But I wanted you to know why I did what I did. It wasn't because I'm a bad friend, or because I didn't care about your feelings."

Lisa winced as she remembered some of the horrible things she'd said to Carole during their fight. "I'm sorry, too," she said. "For the stuff I said, I mean. I know you've been busy." That wasn't an excuse for what Carole had done, but Lisa knew it wouldn't do any good for her to hold a grudge. What had happened had happened, and all they could do now was take it from there. If that meant compromising a little, letting Carole off the hook a bit too easily, so be it. "Anyway, I'm just glad Prancer's not sick." She paused. "Although this twin thing is pretty scary, isn't it?"

Carole nodded. "Sure, but we'll get her through it," she said. "And listen, while we're on the subject of secrets, there's something else I think you should know."

As Lisa shifted in her seat, the fabric of her dress rustled around her legs. Suddenly remembering her promise to her mother, she stood and reached around to unhook the closure in the back. "What is it?" she asked, her voice slightly muffled by the fabric as she slipped the dress off over her head.

"It's something else about Prancer." Carole's voice suddenly sounded brighter. "Something great. Max made me promise not to tell anybody this part, either, but I figure it's the least I owe you after putting you through all that stuff with her pregnancy and everything. . . ."

Still holding the dress, Lisa shook her hair back and stared at Carole. She wasn't sure she was ready for another surprise today. "What is it?"

Carole was grinning. "Max and your dad have been talking for a couple of months now," she said. "It's all arranged. Well, almost, you know, except maybe for some final financial details or whatever. I guess there's no real rush with that, since they weren't going to tell you until your birthday, and I know your dad wants it to be a big surprise, but I thought it would help you get through the next few months while Prancer's out of commission, and so I thought if I told you—"

"Told me what?" Lisa demanded impatiently, clutching the dress so tightly that the fabric started to wrinkle. At times like this, Carole could be awfully aggravating. She tended to talk in circles and interrupt herself so often that whatever she was saying got completely lost in the shuffle. "What are you talking about?"

"Prancer, of course," Carole replied matter-of-factly. "Your dad's going to buy her for you. Once her foals are weaned, she'll be all yours!"

TWO

"Callie's really making great progress, isn't she?" Carole commented, leaning on the fence of Pine Hollow's main outdoor schooling ring. Her gaze was trained on a tall, blond girl aboard a sturdy palomino. Watching Callie Forester riding around the ring on PC right then, it would have been impossible for a stranger to tell that she was still suffering from residual brain damage as the result of a bad car accident. Even Carole was having trouble seeing the weakness in Callie's right side, and she knew exactly what to look for. She had followed the other girl's recovery every step of the way. It was only natural, since she had been in the car at the time of the accident a few months earlier.

Stevie, who was perched on the fence a couple of feet away, nodded. "She's amazing, isn't she?" She shook her head, her voice deep with admiration. "When Callie puts her mind to something, it gets done."

"Of course, we should probably give Emily some of the credit, too," Carole reminded Stevie, glancing at the other rider in the ring with Callie. Their friend Emily Williams had been born with cerebral palsy, and she couldn't walk without crutches. But that hadn't stopped her from becoming an accomplished rider, with a little help from PC, who had been specially trained to compensate for his rider's physical differences. Emily's expertise and support—not to mention her cheerful, unwavering encouragement—had been instrumental in Callie's relatively rapid recovery. At the moment, she was sitting aboard Patch, one of Max's gentlest school horses, watching with rapt attention as Callie cantered around her on PC.

Carole watched the workout in the ring silently for a moment or two. Then Stevie glanced over at her. "By the way," she said, "it was cool what you did yesterday. Going over to apologize to Lisa, I mean. She can be pretty scary when she's mad at someone." She shuddered elaborately. "Believe me, I know."

Carole shrugged. "It wasn't that big a deal," she muttered. She still felt a little bit uncomfortable about the whole incident. Their fight had gone on for longer than she'd quite realized at the time, which probably explained why Stevie seemed so relieved that it was over now. Carole supposed that was partly her fault. She had been terribly upset for the first day or so after the fight, but then, somehow, she had gotten distracted for a couple of days. She figured that probably had something to do with how busy she was at the stable with Samson's training and everything else. And of course, worrying about that stupid history test hadn't helped much, either. In any case, it had taken Lisa's cold glares on Saturday to really bring their problems back to the front of her mind. After stewing about it a little bit longer, she had finally decided that the best thing to do was just to apologize, which seemed to be what Lisa wanted. She had wanted to end this fight before it got any farther out of hand.

Of course, Carole had been pretty angry herself at the time. Lisa had really jumped to conclusions about Carole's intentions, and Carole still didn't think she'd been fair. In fact, her reaction had been downright shocking—she was so even-tempered most of the time that when she really lost it she *could* be pretty scary, as Stevie had put it.

Still, Carole knew better than anyone that horse love could make people do crazy things. And Lisa was definitely crazy about Prancer. She had been in deep horse love practically from the moment she'd first laid eyes on the elegant Thoroughbred mare.

And now Prancer was going to be hers. . . .

Carole still felt a warm glow when she remembered breaking the good news to Lisa the day before. Lisa hadn't really believed her at first, but after countless assurances from Carole that it was the truth, she had been thrilled.

In Carole's opinion, it was long past time that Lisa had her own horse. She couldn't help noticing that Lisa was spending less time at the stable these days. Carole hated the thought that Lisa might be getting too distracted by other things to remember how much she loved riding. Owning a wonderful horse like Prancer would be just the thing to renew her enthusiasm.

She didn't tell Stevie what she was thinking, though. As much as she would have liked to share her excitement about Lisa's wonderful new secret, she thought it should be Lisa's place to break the news. Besides, Stevie wasn't like Lisa—she wouldn't be hurt when she found out that Carole and Lisa had known something she didn't. She would be too busy being excited for Lisa. That was the kind of person she was. She rarely looked on the dark side of things when she had the chance of seeing the bright side.

That reminded Carole of A.J. She had to admit that she hadn't paid much attention to his problems until a few days ago. Even then she had been a little distracted by her fight with Lisa, her plans for Samson's training, and other things. . . .

Like that stupid test, for one, she thought before she could stop herself.

She bit her lip, wishing there were a switch in her mind she could use to turn off her thoughts on that particular subject. The week before, Carole had peeked at her textbook during a makeup history test. She still couldn't even think of the blunt, ugly word for what she'd done—*cheated*—without cringing. She had vowed to put the whole incident behind her, but that wasn't proving to be easy. Thoughts of the test kept popping up at odd times—when she was in the shower, while she was picking out the hooves of her horse, Starlight, and of course every time she walked into history class—and she couldn't do anything to stop them.

To distract herself now, she forced her thoughts back to A.J. "So what's the latest on the A.J. front?" she asked Stevie.

Stevie glanced at her and rolled her eyes. "Who knows?" she said glumly. "The other day was such a disaster, we're not quite sure what to try next."

Stevie sighed as she thought back to the events of Saturday. She and Phil had had such high hopes—they had arranged with A.J.'s parents to have the house to themselves, had gathered most of A.J.'s closest friends—but in the end it hadn't done any good at all. Finally they hadn't had much choice but to give up and leave without any new answers or breakthroughs.

That conclusion hadn't been to Stevie's liking at all. She hated having to sit back helplessly, waiting and wondering, without any way of making things better. She had thought and thought about A.J.'s weird behavior so much for the past few weeks that it sometimes felt as though her thoughts were running on some kind of endlessly repeating loop. At the moment, even hearing his name made her feel weary. She decided it was time to change the subject. Fortunately, she knew an easy way to do that. "So anyway, Carole," she said. "I've been meaning to ask. How's Samson's training going?"

Carole's whole face lit up. "He's great!" she said eagerly. "Today we did some jumping in circles to test his suppleness, and then we practiced his downward transitions for a while, and then we . . ."

Stevie's mind drifted as her friend launched into a detailed description of the technical aspects of Samson's latest training session. Max had asked Carole to take on the big black gelding's training as a special project, and Carole had taken to it the way a horse takes to hay. Samson had been born at Pine Hollow, and Stevie still remembered how brokenhearted Carole had been when Max had sold him a couple of years earlier. The spirited horse had always been special to Carole because she had loved his sire, who'd been killed in a tragic accident long ago, and so it had been harder for her than for anyone to see Samson go. Now that he was back, she really seemed to be trying to make up for lost time. She rarely let an hour pass these days without mentioning her favorite new pupil at least sixty-five times.

Stevie listened patiently to Carole's chattering about transitions and pacing and cavalletti for a few minutes. Finally, when Carole paused for a breath, Stevie broke in. "Sounds great," she said with a grin. "I just hope all this fancy training stuff isn't going to your head. You might get too big for your breeches and think you're too good to muck out stalls with the rest of us peons."

Carole giggled. "That reminds me. My pitchfork awaits. I should get back to work soon."

"But you just got here," Stevie protested. "Come on. Max won't fire you if you relax for an extra two seconds and talk to me. And I was just kidding about mucking out. Really."

"It's not that." Carole flicked at a horsefly that had just landed on the fence in front of her. "I really do have a lot to do today, and Dad's already complaining that he's barely seen me since he got back the other night."

Stevie nodded, remembering that Carole's father, a retired Marine colonel, had recently returned from a weeklong business trip. Colonel Hanson was one of Stevie's favorite people, and she couldn't blame Carole for wanting to hurry home to spend time with him. "Still," she said, "you know what they always say about all work and no play."

Carole grinned. "You're a bad influence," she teased, picking at a hangnail as she spoke. "But seriously, I just came out here to take a five-minute break after I finished grooming Samson. Our training session today went so well that I thought I deserved a little rest before I tackled Starlight's grooming and the rest of my chores for the day."

Stevie opened her mouth to tease Carole about her phrasing—since when had grooming her beloved Starlight become a "chore"?—but before she could speak she heard footsteps on the packed dirt path leading to the ring. Glancing over her shoulder, she saw George Wheeler approaching.

George's family had moved to Willow Creek the year before from downstate. He was in Stevie's grade at Fenton Hall and a regular rider at Pine Hollow, but she didn't know him very well in spite of all that. What she did know was that he was a fantastic rider, though he hardly looked like one. He looked more like a moon-faced eighth-grade tuba player than the accomplished eventer he actually was. Together with his horse, a polished, agile Trakehner mare, he had won countless ribbons at shows all over the region.

"Hey, George," Carole said, briefly glancing at the new arrival before returning her attention to her hangnail.

"Hi." George greeted Stevie and Carole politely in his soft, slightly high-pitched voice. "How's it going?"

Stevie couldn't help grinning. Fortunately George didn't notice—in fact, that was what Stevie was grinning about in the first place. The short, stocky boy's gaze was trained on the action in the ring.

"Not bad," she answered. "We were just watching Callie's session. She's really doing well, don't you think?" She was careful to keep her voice neutral, not wanting George to guess that she was on to him. She had noticed a week or two ago how often George seemed to turn up when Callie was around.

"She's incredible," George replied. His deep-set gray eyes darted toward Stevie and Carole. "I mean, she's been so brave about—you know, the accident and everything. You know."

Stevie swung her boots against the fence post. "Sure," she said agreeably. *It's really too bad,* she thought as George's attention focused on Callie once again. *Callie's not a shallow person or anything, but I really can't see her going for someone like George. Although you never know about some people's taste. . . .*

When she turned to glance appraisingly at Callie, she saw that the therapeutic riding session seemed to be winding down. Callie and Emily were riding slowly toward the gate. Callie's pretty face was flushed pink with exertion, and she looked pleased as she chatted with Emily. Emily wasn't saying much in response for a change, but Stevie didn't think much about that. She was too glad to see that Callie looked happier and more relaxed than she had since that horrible newspaper article had appeared three days earlier. Stevie hadn't known Callie long, but she knew her well enough to know that it would take longer than a few days for the sensitive girl to get over her old friend's betrayal. But at least she didn't seem to be dwelling on it.

Soon the two riders reached the others. "Nice job out there today, Callie," Carole called out encouragingly.

Callie smiled. "Thanks," she said. "I must have woken up on the right side of the bed this morning. First I get an A on my chem lab, thanks to my brilliant lab partner, George"—she tossed a brief, grateful smile at George, who was still standing beside Stevie at the fence—"and now I have the best session in weeks. That one, of course, is thanks in large part to Emily."

"It pays to have friends in the right places,"

Stevie joked. "Especially when those places are all on horseback."

Callie, Carole, and George chuckled. But Stevie noticed that Emily was frowning. It was an unusual expression for her—she always seemed to be smiling or laughing or just generally looking happy. At the moment, however, her face looked as taut and anxious as Stevie had ever seen it.

"Are you okay?" Stevie asked, suddenly concerned.

"Listen, Callie," Emily said abruptly, not bothering to respond to Stevie's question. "We've got to talk. Privately."

Callie looked surprised. "Okay," she said. "Come on, let's take the horses in." She cast a confused glance at Stevie and the others and shrugged slightly.

Emily was usually one of the most forthright, friendly, and outgoing people Stevie knew. It wasn't like her to demand secret meetings with people. She watched curiously as the two girls dismounted carefully, gathered up their crutches from where they had left them near the mounting block, and headed inside with the horses in tow.

"What do you suppose that was all about?" Carole asked after they had gone.

George looked worried. "I hope it isn't, you know, bad news for Callie."

Stevie would have laughed if she hadn't been so

busy wondering about Emily's odd behavior. *George has it bad, all right*, she thought absently. *No doubt about it.*

As she gazed at the stable doors, another figure appeared. It was Ben Marlow, Pine Hollow's youngest full-time stable hand. Stevie wished she could like Ben more, especially since she could tell that Carole liked him a whole lot more than she was willing to admit. But Ben rarely expended much effort to make himself likeable as far as Stevie could tell, at least not as far as mere human beings were concerned. He was much more interested in horses than in people, and he didn't bother to hide it.

Ben was hurrying toward them. "I've been looking for you," he said in his usual brusque manner.

"Me?" Carole stepped forward.

"All of you," Ben replied, his dark eyes flicking from Carole to Stevie and George. "The three of you. Max wants to see you all in his office right away."

"Why?" Stevie asked.

Ben shrugged. "I'm just the messenger," he muttered. "But it's important. So come on."

Stevie gave a perplexed glance to Carole, who shrugged. Then she glanced at George, who looked just as clueless as she felt.

"Come on," Carole said, sounding a bit worried as she turned to follow Ben, who was already striding back toward the stable. "We'd better go see what this is about. You know how Max hates it when we keep him waiting."

THREE

"Intangible, intractable," Alex muttered. "Why does English have to have so many words that sound so much alike? I wish I'd been born speaking some other language. Taking the PSATs in Russian or Swahili or—or Icelandic would probably be a lot easier."

Lisa glanced up from her physics lab notebook and chuckled sympathetically. As much as she loved Alex, she would be the first to admit that he didn't exactly have a long attention span when it came to schoolwork. "I don't know about that," she joked. "If you were taking the test in Iceland, you'd probably have to keep stopping to chip the icicles off your pencil."

She started to return her attention to her own work, but before she could put pen to paper, Alex reached across the table and took her hand. "Maybe we should take a break," he suggested, stroking her palm gently with his thumb. "Go for a walk, maybe get a bite to eat or something."

Lisa sat back in her chair and stretched, taking a deep breath of the warm, musty, faintly leather-and-mothball-scented air. The Willow Creek Public Library had always been one of Lisa's favorite places to study. Its dusty collection of books wasn't exactly exhaustive, but its dim, oak-paneled reading room and creaky wooden furniture had a charm that was missing from the public high school's gleaming modern facility. As a little girl she had imagined the public library to be the kind of place where an old-fashioned princess or sorcerer might have sat reading far into the night. Now it just felt cozy and comfortable and homey, especially when Alex was sitting across the scarred old table from her.

Obviously the room had failed to work its magic on Alex. He looked decidedly restless, and when he got that way, it was next to impossible to get him to focus. "But we just got here," she protested. "And you need to work. The PSATs are coming up a week from Saturday. That doesn't give you much more time to study." She glanced at her physics notebook and swallowed a sigh. "I'll quiz you on the vocab if you want."

"No good." Alex grinned and pointed to the sign above the checkout desk nearby. SILENCE IS GOLDEN, it read. "But you could quiz me if we were taking a walk outside." He gazed at her with that hopeful puppy-dog look he always got when he really wanted something from her.

It was a look she was never able to refuse. "Well . . ." She glanced at her watch. "All right. But just for a few minutes, okay? I really need to get this physics lab written up tonight."

Alex was already gathering up his books and stuffing them into his well-worn leather backpack. "Deal," he promised. "Now come on. This will do you as much good as it will me."

As soon as she stepped through the library door into the crisp, clear autumn afternoon, Lisa decided he was right. It was one of those perfect days when the air was balanced between the cool, clean feeling of fall and the lingering, insistent warmth of the long Virginia summer. Lisa tipped her head back for a moment and closed her eyes, enjoying the sun on her face and the slight breeze in her hair.

Alex's quick kiss brought her eyes flying open again. "Hey," she said with a giggle. "No fair. You sneaked up on me."

"Guilty as charged." Alex did his best to look contrite. "I'd better make it up to you. How's this?" Before she could protest, he grabbed her around the waist and planted another kiss on her lips.

She pushed away after a moment, laughing. One of the many things she loved about Alex was the way the two of them could goof around like this, just being silly and carefree. It was that endearingly playful side of his personality that had helped her overcome her sad and angry feelings after her parents had split up—that, along with his more serious side, the side that had listened and understood and cared.

The two of them set off down the street hand in hand, wandering aimlessly past the old-fashioned storefronts and small office buildings that surrounded the library. Despite her protests, Lisa wasn't really worried about their interrupted studies. Her physics lab report wasn't due until Wednesday, and Alex was in pretty good shape for the PSATs, thanks to a prep course he'd taken over the summer. Besides, she was still feeling good about her mother's improved state of mind. That morning at breakfast Mrs. Atwood had been just as cheerful as the day before. She had even risen early to make pancakes for Lisa before school—something she hadn't done, as far as Lisa could recall, since before Mr. Atwood had moved out.

Maybe Mom's finally turned the corner, she thought hopefully. *Maybe she's finally coming out of her funk once and for all—getting on with her life without Dad, accepting that things have changed and just dealing with it.* She felt her heart lift slightly at the thought, and she sighed happily as she imagined once again having a mother who could take care of herself, who didn't spend most of her days sunk in her own feelings of bitterness and despair.

"What?" Alex glanced down at her, swinging their arms slightly back and forth as they crossed a tiny side street. "What are you thinking about?"

Lisa told him, describing her mother's pleasant new mood—new dress, pancakes, and all. "I just hope it lasts," she added. "Maybe those gripe, er, group therapy sessions really have been doing her some good after all."

"I hope so." Alex kicked at a stone on the sidewalk. "So when do I get to see that hot new dress she bought you?"

"When you take me out someplace nice," Lisa countered with a grin. "Maybe we should go have some fancy dinner in the city to celebrate the great news about Prancer." The night before on the phone, after swearing him to absolute secrecy, Lisa had told Alex what Carole had confided in her. She knew Carole wouldn't really mind—Lisa just had to share the news with someone or she was afraid she might burst. After all these years, it was hard to believe that she was finally getting a horse of her own, and that that horse was going to be Prancer. . . .

Of course first they all had to survive this pregnancy, and Lisa was suspecting she might have more trouble with that than Prancer herself. Twins were quite unusual in horses, and both foals rarely survived, though so far Prancer was still successfully carrying both of hers. Still, at least Lisa now knew that once the mare finally foaled, she would have more to look forward to than watching her baby or babies grow up. She would also be able to look forward to riding and caring for her for the rest of the mare's life.

"So you're finally going to have your own horse after all this time," Alex commented, still swinging her hand back and forth as they strolled. "How's it feel?"

He had asked her that before, when she'd first given him the news. But once again she stopped to think about it before answering. "Mostly good, I guess." She chewed on her lower lip. "But in a way, it makes me more worried than ever about this pregnancy. Makes me feel more responsible for her, I guess."

Alex nodded sympathetically. He hadn't been riding nearly as long as Lisa had, so she knew he didn't understand as much about the risks Prancer faced in this pregnancy as she did. But he understood *her,* and that was just as important. "Well, at least now you have something great to look forward to when it's all over," he said, as if reading her thoughts. He paused for a moment and grinned. "Come to think of it, so do I. I'll get to see Stevie's face when she finds out I've known about it all along."

Lisa chuckled. Despite their lifelong teasing and bickering, Stevie and Alex were closer than most siblings—being twins could do that to you, Lisa supposed. She knew that Alex would never keep anything truly important from Stevie, nor she from him. The news about Prancer was different, though, because it was something that Stevie didn't really *need* to know right away, since it didn't affect her directly. And Alex knew as well as Lisa did that Stevie would find out about it soon enough. Stevie might pretend to be annoyed with them for keeping it from her, but deep down she wouldn't really mind.

That was all very well and good. But then there was the other secret, the much more important one—or so it seemed to Lisa—that she had asked Stevie to keep from Alex, at least temporarily, until she found a way to tell him herself. She sighed, annoyed at herself for putting it off for so long. She wasn't normally a procrastinator, but somehow the right moment had just never presented itself.

Right now definitely isn't the right moment, either, Lisa told herself as she glanced quickly up at Alex's familiar, contented, adorable face. She felt a bit uncomfortable for putting off the difficult discussion once again. But every time she was alone with Alex, she found herself veering away from this particular topic, like a nervous horse shying at a frightening new object.

Rather than stewing over it any longer, she decided to change the subject. "So, I haven't asked you," she said. "How were things at school today for Scott and Callie?" It was Monday, the Foresters' first day back at Fenton Hall since the article had appeared in the newspaper on Saturday. Lisa attended Willow Creek's public high school, so she hadn't gotten to observe the reactions firsthand, though she had thought of Callie and Scott often during the day.

Alex shook his head. "About how you'd expect," he reported. "A lot of people seem to believe everything they read in the papers. That means a lot of them suddenly think Scott's some kind of binge-drinking alcoholic."

Lisa winced on Scott's behalf. One of the secrets Callie's so-called friend had revealed was that Callie had once caught Scott sneaking a bottle of Scotch out of their parents' liquor cabinet. Personally, Lisa thought it had probably been just one of those experimental things that a lot of kids did—an isolated incident, not a habit. She had known Scott for only a short time, but he hadn't shown any signs of a drinking problem, and as far as Lisa was concerned, that meant he was innocent until proven guilty.

"As for Callie," Alex went on, "well, let's just say her days of anonymity are over."

Lisa raised one eyebrow. "Anonymity?" she joked. "Do my ears deceive me, or did you just use one of your PSAT words in a sentence?"

Alex stuck out his tongue at her. "Bleah," he said. "You would have to bring up the PSATs just when we were having such a nice time."

Lisa laughed, then shivered as a cool breeze tickled the back of her neck. "Brr!" she said, shaking off the sudden chill. "It's really starting to get cooler in the afternoons these days."

"I thought fall was your favorite season."

"It is." Lisa shrugged. "I wasn't really complaining. I love fall—the leaves turn all those gorgeous colors, there's that nice crispness to the air, the apples are ripe. . . ."

"Football season starts," Alex picked up. "And soccer season. Oh, and of course there's Halloween, just a few short weeks away now." He let out a ghostly cackle. "Now, that's really something to love about the fall."

Lisa rolled her eyes. Halloween was a popular holiday in the Lake family. When they were a little younger, Stevie, Alex, and their two brothers had expended a lot of energy competing with each other to come up with the scariest costumes and most ghoulish practical jokes. "True," she said. "But if we're talking fall holidays, I'll take

Thanksgiving every time." Flashing onto an image of her mother scowling into the oven and muttering about how she had no idea how to carve a turkey because she'd never had to do it before, she shuddered slightly. "Even now."

Alex shot her another sympathetic look, immediately guessing what she was thinking. "At least last year your aunt and her family came down," he said. "Maybe they'll do that again this—Hey!" He grinned. "Forget your aunt. Why don't you and your mom come over to my house for Turkey Day this year?"

Lisa was already wishing she'd never brought up the subject. Her father had called the week before to invite her to spend the holiday in California. She hadn't given him an answer yet, mostly because she couldn't bear the thought of leaving her mother to fend for herself on such a family-oriented holiday. But if her aunt invited her mother up to New Jersey, there was no reason Lisa had to go along . . .

"You're sweet to offer," she told Alex lightly. "But Thanksgiving's a long way away yet. Why worry about making plans now?"

"It's not that far away," Alex insisted, turning to face her and grasping both her hands. "Just think—we could spend the whole day together stuffing our faces and watching football on TV. Wouldn't that be awesome? And you know my

42

parents would love to have you. So would Stevie. And Chad will be home, of course. You can talk to him about campus life at UNV. You're still planning to apply there, aren't you?"

Lisa's head was spinning. How did one little secret manage to make everything so complicated? And why did Alex have to bring up the topic of college applications when she was already feeling so anxious about her secret from the summer? It was true that she planned to apply to the University of Northern Virginia, a college about forty miles from Willow Creek where Alex's older brother, Chad, was a sophomore. But she'd also sent away for applications from a number of other schools, including a few she hadn't quite mentioned to Alex yet—particularly the ones in California.

She knew that Alex wanted what was best for her. He really did. But he also wanted to be with her as much of the time as possible, and he couldn't seem to get it through his head that the two things might not be totally compatible. Though he had always seemed to understand just about everything else about her, he had never really understood her decision to spend the summer in California. He'd seen it as a choice she had made to go *away* from him, rather than seeing that she might be going *toward* something else— like her father, her baby half sister, an exciting summer job, a new experience. All he had been able or willing to focus on was that the two of them would be apart for more than two months, which made her think that it would be even more difficult for him to accept the possibility that she could choose to be away from him for four whole years when there was a good school like UNV so close by. Lisa didn't much like the thought of a long-distance relationship either, but she could accept that it might be a necessity, at least for a while. She wanted to choose the college that would be the right one for her, would prepare her best for the rest of her life. And what was four years in comparison to her whole life, their whole lives together? *A long time,* she admitted reluctantly. Still, she wished Alex would at least try to understand.

Meanwhile, he was still waiting for a response to his invitation. "Let me think about it, okay?" Lisa said. "And I'll need to talk to Mom, of course. I'm afraid she may have her heart set on going up to New Jersey this year."

Alex shrugged. "Sure. But while you're thinking about it, don't forget to think about how totally romantic it would be to snuggle together on the couch in the den, feeding each other little bits of pumpkin pie. . . ." He leaned over and playfully kissed her on the earlobe, then on the cheek.

For a moment, Lisa's worries and secrets disappeared and she pushed him away, giggling. "That doesn't sound romantic at all," she said. "I hate pumpkin pie, remember?" She giggled again as, undeterred, he grabbed her around the waist and planted a big, wet kiss right on her nose. "Okay, okay," she said. "Make it apple, and we can talk."

Just then there was an unpleasant interruption. Somewhere nearby, a loud, whiny voice let out a shriek and cried, "I can't believe you!"

"Please, you have to listen to me," a male voice pleaded. "I tried, I really did. My cousin said he could get the tickets, but he totally bailed on me at the last minute."

The first voice clearly wasn't impressed by that argument. "*Whatever*," it said coldly. "I'm not interested in your little family dramas. All I'm interested in is the fact that, apparently, I still don't have tickets for the fall festival this weekend."

Lisa pulled away from Alex reluctantly. "Is that who I think it is?" she commented, glancing down the street in the direction of the voice.

"Sounds like Veronica's about to dump another boyfriend," Alex replied with a smirk.

Lisa spotted Veronica diAngelo, a girl their age, standing at the end of the block. Veronica tended to be noticeable in just about any situation—she was tall and slender, with sleek dark hair, a lovely if slightly haughty face, and a self-confident way of carrying herself that made most people sit up and take notice. In this case, she was even more conspicuous than usual. Fury radiated from her. She was standing with her arms crossed over her light cashmere sweater, glaring at a tall, handsome boy with thick black hair. He looked sheepish and kept glancing around nervously as if searching for a way out.

Lisa couldn't blame him. Veronica diAngelo had never been one of her favorite people, and she was even more insufferable than usual when she was angry about something. "So the Princess of Virginia doesn't get to go to the big fall concert," Lisa murmured to Alex. "Makes me wish even more I'd been able to get tickets." Just about everyone she knew wanted to go to the annual show in neighboring Berryville, which featured several popular local bands. But the seats in the town's only concert hall were limited and tickets were hard to come by. Lisa had done her best, even calling in a few times to radio station giveaways, but with no luck.

Veronica was so busy berating her apparently soon-to-be-ex-boyfriend that she didn't seem to notice she was attracting an audience. In addition to Lisa and Alex, several other passersby had stopped to stare.

"Maybe someone will take pity on that poor dumb guy and give their tickets to Veronica," Lisa joked quietly. Then she shrugged. "Probably not, though. If I had tickets, there's no way I'd give them up. Besides, any guy who voluntarily dates Veronica deserves what he gets."

"And a lobotomy," Alex whispered. "Come on, let's get lost before she spots us and decides to start spreading the love around." He wrapped one arm around Lisa's shoulder and jerked his head to indicate their escape route.

Lisa giggled and nodded, allowing him to steer her off down the sidewalk at a fast trot. Seeing Veronica with the latest in her long line of male companions made Lisa appreciate even more what she and Alex had together.

Maybe he can't get me tickets to the fall festival either, she thought with a secret smile. *But I don't mind. As long as we're together, that's all the festivity I need.*

FOUR

Carole fidgeted and tried not to stare at the clock above the desk. She was leaning against the table near the office door waiting for Max to show up. Stevie was sitting in the single chair in front of the desk, while Ben and George stood against the side wall. Ben looked as inscrutable as ever, but the others' expressions reflected the same curiosity that Carole herself was feeling.

But perhaps not quite the same amount of impatience. Every minute they sat there twiddling their thumbs was a minute she could have been spending getting her chores done. She still had to sweep the stable aisles and make her monthly check of the human and equine first-aid kits kept in the student locker room and the tack room. Plus she would have to help Ben bring in the horses that had been turned out in the pasture for the day, along with the million or so other tasks that always seemed to require her urgent attention . . .

As she was counting up the number of stalls she would probably have to muck out that afternoon, Max came rushing into the office, breathless and apologetic.

"I had to run out for a second to help Denise with that hyper new filly that's boarding here," he explained, taking a seat behind the desk. Denise McCaskill was the assistant manager at Pine Hollow. "I was hoping she could be here for this—Denise, that is, not the filly—but she's going to be tied up for a while yet."

"That's okay," Stevie said trying to appear casual. "So what's your big news?"

Max smiled and glanced at Ben. "Ben already knows," he said. "I asked him not to give it away, and I guess he didn't, since I know Stevie wouldn't be looking so calm right now if she knew."

"Give what away?" Stevie demanded as Carole glanced curiously at Ben. He was staring at the toes of his work boots, his expression neutral.

Max tapped his fingers on the wooden desktop, the corners of his mouth twitching slightly the way they always did when he was trying to suppress a smile. "I suppose you've all heard about the upcoming Colesford Horse Show by now."

"Of course we— What!" Stevie exclaimed. "This is about the Colesford Horse Show? What? *What?*"

"Colesford!" George murmured in awe, looking almost as curious as Stevie.

Carole was intrigued. She had been hearing about the Colesford Horse Show for some time now. It was being held in a nearby town the following month, and it promised to be one of the most prestigious, most competitive shows on the East Coast. She held her breath, hardly daring to hope that Max was about to say what she thought he might be about to say. *Could he . . . ? Would he . . . ?*

Max was grinning openly by now, clearly enjoying the expressions on the faces of the riders in front of him. Even Ben looked amused as he leaned back against the wall near the door, his arms crossed over his chest.

"Right," Max said briskly, still grinning. "You see, I've been going over the stable's finances, and it seems we've had a very good year so far. Of course, we can always use a few more students and boarders, and the best way to attract them is with good publicity. That's why I figured out that I can afford to send exactly five of my current riders to Colesford next month. I thought I could sponsor these five on the condition that they ride under the Pine Hollow name, represent the stable to the best of their considerable abilities, and—"

Carole quickly did the math. But Stevie was faster.

"You mean us?" she cried, sounding excited. "All of us?" She turned halfway around in her seat as if unwilling to believe it until she counted again. "Carole, Ben, Denise, George—and me?"

Carole grinned at her friend's excitement. She was feeling pretty thrilled herself.

Colesford! she thought in amazement. *I'm actually going to be riding at Colesford. But is Starlight ready for*—She cut off the thought as she realized that Max was speaking again.

". . . and of course, you'll be riding Belle," he was telling Stevie. "I think you have the best shot if you stick to dressage."

Stevie nodded. "Sounds great."

Max turned to George next. "You and Joyride should be able to do well in a few different events. We can meet separately after you've had a chance to think it over and discuss which ones you want to enter."

George nodded, his eyes shining. His specialty was three-day eventing, so Carole guessed he'd probably end up entering some dressage classes and some jumping ones. "Sure," he said. "Thanks, Max."

"Ben, as I told you before, I'd like you to ride Topside for this show," Max went on, glancing at the young stable hand. Carole nodded, impressed with the pairing. The Thoroughbred gelding had been a top-notch competitor in his younger days,

51

and he would still be a formidable competitor at Colesford—especially with an excellent rider like Ben in the saddle. "He hasn't competed in a few months," Max added, "but he's in excellent shape, so if you put in some work with him between now and the show I think you'll do fine."

"Who's Denise riding?" Stevie interrupted. "Let me guess—Talisman, right?"

Max seemed uncertain whether or not to be annoyed at the interruption. He nodded. "That's right," he said. "They've always worked well together."

Carole realized she was holding her breath as Max turned to face her. Would he think Starlight was ready for a major competition like this? Or . . .

"Carole," Max pronounced, "I hope you're not going to be disappointed by my suggestion." He paused and stroked his chin thoughtfully.

"What is it, Max?" she asked a bit apprehensively.

He rubbed his callused hands together and gazed at her solemnly. "I know Starlight is a wonderful horse, and you've done some incredible work with him over the years. But I'm still not sure he'd be up to the competition at Colesford. How would you feel about riding Samson in the show instead? He could use the experience, and I think—"

"I'll do it!" Carole exclaimed. She could hardly believe her luck. It was as if Max had been reading her mind. "I'll do it!"

"Guess what, girl!" Stevie exclaimed as she let herself into her horse's stall. "We're hitting the big time!"

Belle seemed unimpressed with the news. She swung her big bay head around to look at Stevie, continuing all the while to chew diligently on the mouthful of hay she'd just pulled from her rack.

Stevie gave the mare a hearty pat on her sleek neck. "There's no need to look so snooty about it," she told the horse. "You know as well as I do that we should bow down and kiss the ground Max walks on for giving us this opportunity."

She was only half kidding. While she took her dressage training seriously and was good at it, she was realistic enough to know that she was the least likely of all the Pine Hollow entrants to wind up with any sort of ribbon, and she really did appreciate Max's faith in her abilities. Even to compete at Colesford would be an honor, whether she won best in show or came in dead last in every class she entered.

"Not that I'm planning to do that, of course," she murmured, running her fingers through Belle's silky mane. Stevie had a competitive streak as wide as Pine Hollow's big south pasture, a quality that had caused her some trouble in the past. In her younger days, she had often gotten so carried away with the idea of winning that she hurt people's feelings or forgot about other priorities.

Over the past few years, however, she had matured enough to have a sense of humor about her own competitiveness. She still liked to win, but she realized that not every contest had to be a battle to the death, and that losing out on the grand prize once in a while made the triumphs, when they came, that much more satisfying.

"Anyway," she said, looking deep into Belle's liquid brown eyes, "even though Max didn't say so, I'll bet he was planning on making Andrea the fifth member of his little team." Andrea Barry was a sophomore at Willow Creek High School and one of the most talented riders at Pine Hollow. She and her athletic hunter gelding, Country Doctor, had often competed in shows almost as prestigious and competitive as Colesford. "I guess it's lucky for us she came down with mono last week, huh?"

Belle let out a snort and a snuffle, then turned her head to grab another mouthful of hay. Stevie took a few steps back to give her room.

"I know, I know," she said with a chuckle. "That's not a very nice thing to say." She leaned back against the wall and grinned, hugging herself in pure excitement. "But I can't help it. It's going to be awesome!"

At that same moment, Carole was hurrying down Pine Hollow's U-shaped stable aisle toward Samson's stall. Her mind was full to bursting with Max's news. It was thrilling enough that she would be riding at Colesford at all. To be going there as a team with Samson . . .

"Incredible," she whispered aloud, still hardly believing her luck. Samson had already won quite a few ribbons with his last owner. And he seemed to get faster and stronger and smarter every day that Carole worked with him. There was no telling what he could do, how well he could perform. More importantly, this show would be the best test Carole could imagine of the training she'd done so far. Working alone or with one or two of Pine Hollow's other horses was fine, but it could only tell her so much. Riding Samson under the pressure of a real show—with dozens of other horses, an audience, and judges watching their every move—would be a true learning experience for both of them. For the two of them as a team.

It's going to be totally amazing, she thought as she rounded the corner and spotted Samson's familiar black head sticking out of his stall halfway down the aisle. As usual, she smiled as soon as she saw him. *How did I get to be so lucky? I must be doing something right!*

Despite her ebullient mood, that last thought struck a deep chord in her heart. Unbidden, the image of the big red *F* marked at the top of her history test floated into her mind.

Forget about that stupid test, she told herself angrily, shaking her head as if she could shake the memory right out of it. *You did what you had to do. If you hadn't, you wouldn't be standing here right now as an official entrant in the Colesford Horse Show.*

That much was true enough. Carole never could have passed that makeup test without cheating, and if she hadn't passed, her grade average for the class would have dropped below Max's cutoff point. Every student had to maintain a C average or lose riding privileges until his or her grades came up, and Carole couldn't bear the thought of being banned from her favorite place in the entire world for something as minor as one stupid history test.

Still, all the rationalization in the world couldn't make her feel easy about what she'd done. Fortunately, she knew one surefire way to take her mind off it. Jogging the last few steps to Samson's stall, she gave him a welcoming pat on his soft nose and reached for the latch on the door.

"Carole."

The voice startled her so much that she jumped and let out an involuntary *"Eeep!"* She hadn't realized anyone else—well, anyone on two legs—was in the aisle. She turned and saw Callie standing in the shadow of a support beam a few yards down the aisle.

"Sorry if I scared you," Callie said quietly.

"That's okay." Carole smiled. "I guess I was kind of distracted. Hey, you'll never guess what Max wanted to talk to us ab— What's wrong?"

She had just noticed that Callie's blue eyes were red-rimmed and her face was taut and grim. Her knuckles were white as they clenched and unclenched rhythmically on the handles of her metal crutches.

Callie tossed her head, sending her blond hair flying out of her eyes. "Do you know where Stevie is?" she asked. "I don't want to have to repeat this more than I have to."

"With Belle, I think," Carole said automatically, still staring at Callie. "Does this have something to do with that horrible article?"

"No, it's not that." Callie was already moving off down the aisle toward Belle's stall. "Come on."

Carole followed, worried and mystified. Callie wasn't usually the dramatic type, and she certainly wasn't the type to wallow in her own misery in front of other people. So what could have happened in the time since they'd left her? She and Stevie and the others had only been in Max's office a few minutes.

Carole could hear Stevie chattering away at her horse as she and Callie approached. As far as she could tell, Stevie seemed to be explaining the complexities of show grooming and etiquette to Belle.

At Carole's knock, Stevie stuck her head out over the stall's half door. "Hi, guys," she said, pushing a strand of dark blond hair out of her eyes with the back of her hand. "What's up?"

"Callie has something she wants to tell us," Carole said.

Callie glanced up and down the aisle to make sure they were alone. Then she leaned heavily on her crutches and gazed solemnly at Stevie and Carole.

"It's about Emily," she said, her voice breaking slightly on the name. "She just told me. She's moving. To Australia."

FIVE

Stevie twirled the combination lock on her gym locker expertly. Yanking open the door, she tossed her shoes inside and began digging for a clean T-shirt and pair of shorts. "But really," she said without looking around. "You can't help being a *teensy* bit excited for her, right?"

Behind her, she heard Callie sigh. "I know. You're right. If she has to move at all, it's pretty cool that she's moving to Australia. I was there once, and it's awesome—the people are super nice."

Stevie shook her head in amazement. Callie had led quite a life as the daughter of a successful politician. She'd probably been to more interesting places than Stevie could even imagine. Still, Stevie knew there were plenty of trade-offs. In exchange for their interesting, glamorous lifestyle, Callie and her family had given up an awful lot of their privacy.

"I think Emily's really going to like it there,"

Callie went on. "When she gave me the news, I could tell she was already nervous. But I could also tell she was kind of excited, but that she didn't want me to see that and feel bad . . . you know."

"I know." Stevie pulled off her light cotton sweater and tossed it into her locker. Reaching for the only slightly rumpled T-shirt she'd found, she thought about Emily's big news. When Callie had first told her and Carole the day before, Stevie had hardly been able to believe that their friend was really moving halfway around the world. But now it was finally starting to sink in. Emily's father's company had transferred him to Sydney, and her mother, who worked for the government, had managed to line up a job at the American embassy there.

"Is that what the lunch thing with her parents last Saturday was all about?" Stevie asked when her head emerged from the neck of her T-shirt.

Callie nodded. "That's why she couldn't come with us, remember? They told her the news over lunch."

"Wow." Stevie couldn't imagine how she would react if her parents ever dropped such a bombshell on her. Still, she couldn't help shivering a little with excitement on Emily's behalf. Australia! Kangaroos, the outback, crocodiles and dingoes and didgeridoos—it sounded so exotic, so interesting and cool. . . .

Suddenly she noticed that Callie didn't look excited at all. She just looked sad.

It must be tough for her, Stevie thought as she pulled her sneakers out of the bottom of her locker. *She hasn't known Emily anywhere near as long as the rest of us, but she'll probably miss her even more than we do because of her physical therapy. She tries to be so tough and independent and everything, but it's obvious that she totally relies on Emily when it comes to that.*

"How come they're leaving PC here?" she asked. "I know they're pretty strict over there, because of all the problems they've had with imported species endangering native plants and animals."

Callie nodded. "There are major quarantine rules." She gave Stevie a sidelong glance. "Actually, horses aren't even native to the continent. Did you know that?"

"I think I did," Stevie replied, jamming her feet into her sneakers and leaning over to tie the laces. "I seem to remember Carole telling me something like that when she was on one of her international horse-information kicks."

Callie smiled slyly. "But did she tell you how the equestrian events for the Melbourne Olympics—I think that was back in the 1950s sometime—had to be held in Sweden because of Australia's regulations?"

Stevie shrugged. "Of course." Then she grinned. "Okay, I'm lying. I don't remember her telling me that. But she probably did." She finished tying her laces and sat up, glancing at Callie. "Sometimes when Carole's on a roll with one of her horse-related lectures, it's hard to take in every single thing she says."

Callie laughed out loud at that. "Right. But in any case, I don't think the quarantine stuff is the main reason Emily decided to donate PC back to Free Rein." That was the name of the therapeutic riding center where Emily had learned to ride and where she had first paired up with PC. "She's going to look for another horse when she gets over there—she's pretty excited about having a chance to help train it herself."

Stevie stood and slammed her locker door. "Sounds like fun. And Free Rein will be thrilled to have PC." Secretly, she was a bit surprised that Emily was so eager to get rid of the horse she'd ridden for so many years. She knew that Emily wasn't particularly sentimental, but Stevie herself couldn't imagine just tossing Belle aside if her family moved—or for any other reason. The two of them were a team, just as Emily and PC had always been a team.

As if reading her mind, Callie continued. "Emily knows that PC will be appreciated at Free Rein," she said. "Plus she's trying to consider what's best for the horse. PC's not old, but he's not exactly young, either."

"Oh." Stevie hadn't thought about it from that point of view before. "Shipping him all that way would probably be tough on him, wouldn't it?"

Callie nodded. "I'm sure he'd adjust. But Emily still doesn't want to put him through all that. Not to mention making her family take on the shipping expenses, and the cost and hassle of all the special vet stuff they'd have to go through before and after quarantine. . . ."

Stevie nodded slowly. It all made sense in a way, though she wasn't sure she could ever come to the same decision if she and Belle were put in a similar situation. Still, she knew that Emily had never been afraid to embrace change or new opportunities. "Sounds like she made the mature choice," she mused aloud.

Callie leaned back against a locker. "I'm sure PC will miss her, but he'll get over it," she said. "I just hope the rest of us can, too."

Stevie shot Callie a sympathetic look. Once again, she realized that the other girl was upset about losing her therapeutic riding coach. But in her usual self-sufficient way, she was trying not to let it show. "We'll never stop missing her." She shrugged and grinned. "But look on the bright side. Now that we'll have a friend to stay with in Australia, there's that much more chance our parents will decide to let us all go!"

Callie laughed. "Right," she said. "What's a couple of thou for the airfare when we have a free place to crash?"

Callie was still thinking about Emily's move as she and Stevie walked out of the locker room into the gym. Because of her crutches, she had been excused from participating in phys ed this semester, but that didn't mean she was excused from attending. Ever since school had started at the beginning of September, she had been sitting in the bleachers, bored out of her mind for forty minutes twice a week, watching her classmates jog or do sit-ups or play dodgeball.

The last day and a half made her long for those dull days. Since that idiotic article had appeared in the national press, she and Scott had been the talk of the school. She was sure that today's phys ed class was going to be no exception.

As she entered the gym, whispers were audible above the hollow bouncing of basketballs and the squeaking of dozens of sneakers. Almost every one of her classmates turned to look at her curiously as she walked past on her crutches. Most of them were obviously trying not to look as though they were staring. But one girl—one tall, pretty girl with long, straight dark hair—was staring openly. As Callie averted her eyes, the girl smiled and started toward her.

"Uh-oh," Stevie murmured in her ear. "Veronica alert."

It was too late for Callie to respond or try to escape. She pasted her most convincing fake smile on her face as Veronica reached them.

"Hi, Callie," Veronica said brightly. "How's it going?"

Callie shrugged, feeling suspicious. Veronica was the leader of the most popular clique of juniors and seniors at Fenton Hall. She had always been cool at best to Callie in the past, when she had bothered to acknowledge her existence at all. "It's going," she replied cautiously.

"Right," Stevie added. "I guess that means *you* should be going, Veronica."

Callie winced. She knew that Stevie and Veronica had never gotten along—she'd heard enough hair-raising stories about the stunts they'd pulled on each other to leave no doubt in her mind about that. Still, she sometimes wished that Stevie could be a little more tactful—a little less blunt in expressing herself. Callie never hesitated to stand up for herself, but she didn't like the sorts of unnecessary confrontations the other girl seemed to thrive on. If only Stevie could develop a little more . . . *finesse*. It was one of Callie's mother's favorite words.

Fortunately, Veronica didn't take the slightest notice of Stevie's comment. She was still gazing at Callie with that smile on her face. Callie noticed that her lip gloss exactly matched the shade of her T-shirt. "Okay," Veronica said cheerfully. "Well, I just wanted to make sure you were okay. I mean, being in that accident and all must have been kind of rough."

"Well, that all seems like ages ago now," Callie said lightly. "But thanks."

"And that newspaper article," Veronica continued. "It must have made things just awful for your father—your whole family." She leaned a little closer. "I just wanted to let you know, Callie, if you need someone to talk to, I'm here for you. I understand how difficult it can be, coming from a prominent family."

Stevie couldn't help letting out an inelegant snort. Veronica's family might be one of the wealthiest in Willow Creek, but that hardly put them in the same league as the Foresters. She could hardly believe the load of manure Veronica was shoveling out at the moment. Did she really think Callie was going to forget that she had spent the past four or five weeks ignoring her at best, insulting her at worst?

Obviously she did. She didn't bother to acknowledge Stevie's snort as she continued to stare empathetically at Callie. And Callie was smiling back as if this conversation were the most normal thing in the world.

Stevie knew how Veronica's shallow, self-involved little mind worked well enough to see straight through her, even if Callie couldn't. *Veronica must have just realized that Congressman Forester is a prominent member of the House, and that in her own pathetic, feeble set of priorities that makes Callie someone worth knowing,* she thought in disgust.

At that moment one of Veronica's friends called to her, and Veronica excused herself—to Callie, again ignoring Stevie—and hurried away. Callie let out a long sigh when she was gone.

"Wow," she said quietly. "Talk about Dr. Jekyll and Mr. Hyde. I'm not sure which of her personalities is worse."

Stevie let out her own sigh of relief. She was glad Callie hadn't fallen for Veronica's about-face. "Tell me about it. Now that you're on her friendship list, she'll make your life a living hell until you agree to be her best friend forever." She shrugged. "The best thing to do is just tell her right now that you'll never be friends with such a sniveling, spiteful, self-absorbed princess in a million years, so she can just forget it."

Callie laughed, looking a bit uncomfortable.

"Very funny, Stevie," she said. "I'm sure it won't be that bad."

Before Stevie could explain that she hadn't been joking, the phys ed teacher blew her whistle to start class, ending the discussion.

"Toss me the tomato sauce, will you, sweetie?" Lisa said.

Alex grabbed the open can of sauce from the Atwoods' kitchen counter and pretended he was about to lob it across the room. Lisa held up her hands to shield her face, laughing.

The two of them had been busy for the past half hour fixing dinner—fettuccine with tomato and mushroom sauce. Mrs. Atwood was due home from work at any moment, and Lisa was hoping that by surprising her mother with her favorite meal, she might extend her good mood for one more day at least. It had already lasted a lot longer than Lisa had dared to hope—almost forty-eight hours now!—making their house more peaceful and pleasant to live in than it had been for ages.

Lisa stepped over and attempted to grab the tomato sauce out of Alex's hand. "Give me that," she commanded. "Otherwise I'll send you home without any dinner." She giggled as he pretended to take a sip out of the can before letting her wrestle it away from him.

"I'm glad you're in such a good mood," Alex told her, his face growing more serious. "I was afraid you'd be upset because Stevie and Carole are both going to be in that horse show and Max didn't ask you."

Lisa shrugged. "I probably should be," she admitted, picking up a fork to check the pasta that was bubbling away on the stove. "But all I keep thinking about is how much work they're going to have to do between now and then to be ready for such an important show. I'm thrilled for them, but believe me, I'll be much happier in the stands cheering them on. Denise and George, too. And Ben."

She had almost forgotten to add the moody stable hand to the list. Ben had that effect on her—he tried so hard to be invisible and keep to himself that Lisa often simply forgot he was around. Still, when she did remember to think about it, she had to admit that he was an excellent rider—probably as good as Carole. He had an easy, natural rapport with horses that was really special. He and Topside would be a tough team to beat at the show.

"Anyway," she said, "it's not like I have a competitive horse to enter the show on. Even Starlight wasn't up to the task, remember?"

"If Prancer weren't pregnant . . ."

"She wouldn't be up to it, either," Lisa admitted. As much as she loved the beautiful bay mare, she would be the first to admit that she would probably never win any blue ribbons at a show like Colesford. While her Thoroughbred breeding could probably rival any horse's entered, Prancer simply hadn't received the intensive show-ring training required to compete at that level. "This isn't some casual little Pine Hollow show. The horses there will be tough—really tough."

"I know." Alex reached around her for the salt shaker. "Stevie isn't bragging about how she's going to win every ribbon, like she usually does before these things. She's actually being sort of humble for a change—you know, that 'it's an honor just to be nominated' sort of thing."

Lisa chuckled. "Still, I bet secretly she's at least a *tiny* bit pleased with herself because she's going to be riding at Colesford and Phil isn't." Stevie and her boyfriend had a long history of intense competition. For some reason, Phil had always seemed to bring out the worst in Stevie when they were rivals for anything, no matter how minor. When they were younger, that had threatened their relationship more than once. With age and experience, they had both mellowed enough so that they could enjoy a friendly game of tennis or touch football without turning it into a blood sport.

Glancing over at Alex, Lisa couldn't imagine

wanting to beat him out for anything. She wanted only the best for him, as he did for her. That was what their relationship was all about.

"I'm sure you're right," Alex said. "But I'm sure Phil will be there in the audience, cheering her on with the rest of us."

"True." Lisa paused to test the pasta once more. It still wasn't done, so she set down her fork and glanced at Alex. "I wonder if A.J. will be there, too," she said softly.

Alex reached over and gently squeezed her upper arm. "Seeing him the other day really freaked you out, didn't it?" he said. "Me too."

Lisa nodded. A.J. had been on her mind more and more these past few days. Now that all the surprises regarding Prancer seemed to be out in the open, she actually had some energy to spend thinking about other things—starting with how a nice, funny, outgoing guy like A.J. had suddenly transformed into such a monster.

"What could be going on with him?" Lisa bit her lip and glanced at Alex. "Do you really think it's drugs?"

Alex shrugged. "The more time passes, the more it seems like that's the only thing it could be," he said heavily. "It's hard to believe something like that about A.J., but, well . . ."

Lisa knew what he meant. It was horrible to think that any friend of theirs, especially A.J., could have gotten himself mixed up in something so stupid and dangerous. But what else could make him change so drastically, so suddenly, from the person they knew into a complete stranger?

"We've got to help him somehow," she murmured, more to herself than to Alex. "We've got to find a way to get through to him."

"How can we if he won't even talk to us?" Alex asked.

"Let's think about this." Lisa paused and thought, stirring the spaghetti sauce slowly with a wooden spoon. She'd been speaking casually when she'd brought up A.J.'s name. But now that she really thought about it, she realized that she—and most of the others, she suspected—had been relying on Phil and Stevie to come up with a plan to help A.J. In a way, that was only natural, since they were the closest to him. But now she couldn't help thinking that maybe they were a little *too* close. Maybe their affection and concern for A.J. were keeping them from thinking clearly about all their options.

Besides, we should all be doing whatever we can to help, Lisa told herself. *Isn't that what friends are for?*

She shared what she was thinking with Alex. "So how about it?" she said when she was finished. "Let's try to come up with a new plan."

Alex nodded agreeably. "Okay," he said. "But I

have to admit, I thought the last idea was a pretty good one."

"Me too." Lisa continued to stir the sauce automatically as she turned over the problem in her mind. "But let's be logical about this. Why didn't it work? Why wouldn't he talk to us? What was the problem?"

Alex leaned against the counter. "Obvious," he said. "A.J. got away before we could even try to talk to him."

"And Phil has already tried the one-on-one approach," Lisa said thoughtfully. "I suppose one person is just too easy to ignore, even if it is your best friend."

"Maybe we should send Stevie over there alone." Alex grinned. "If we locked her and A.J. in a room together and just let her talk his ear off, he'd be sure to crack. Of course, it might kill him—"

"That's it!" Lisa cried suddenly. With Alex's words, the perfect plan had come to her in a flash.

"What? You want to kill him?"

"Of course not." Lisa waved a hand impatiently. "It was what you said about locking him in a room so he couldn't get away. That was really the reason why everything went wrong—he got away. You said it yourself."

"Right." Alex looked uncertain. "So what do

you want to do? Wait for him in his room this time?"

"I don't think so." Now that she'd thought of it, the solution seemed so obvious that she couldn't believe none of them had hit on it before. "But we should try again someplace where it's not quite so easy for him to escape. I don't think his house is the answer, though. In case it doesn't work, it's probably not a good idea to have his parents involved."

Alex nodded. "If he decides they're out to get him, he may just take off or something."

Lisa shuddered. That wasn't quite what she'd been thinking—she had just thought that he might not open up as easily or talk as freely if his mother and father were present, especially if his problem had something to do with drugs or drinking or shoplifting or anything else that could be considered scandalous. It was horrible—no, downright *impossible*—to imagine A.J. running away from home. But it was just as impossible to imagine him acting the way he'd been acting for the past few weeks.

"Right," she said, swallowing the lump that had suddenly formed in her throat. "Anyway, I was thinking that someplace more neutral would be better. But it has to be somewhere he goes on a regular basis. That way he'll never see it coming."

Alex nodded. "The element of surprise," he

said. "But where were you thinking of? I mean, we can't all cut last period to wait for him outside his school . . . can we?" he added with a sidelong glance at her.

She shook her head firmly. "No," she said. Lisa had never cut a class in her life, and she wasn't about to start now. "School's no good anyway. Too many other people around."

"And it's not as if A.J. goes there every day anymore, anyway," Alex added ruefully. "Phil told Stevie he skipped again today."

"Well, there's still one place he goes regularly, at least according to something Stevie said a few days ago," Lisa said. "Cross County Stables."

"Aha!" Alex's eyes lit up. "You mean he's still taking care of Crystal? I guess maybe there's hope for him yet."

Lisa nodded. When A.J. had first owned his sweet gray mare, he'd kept her in the small, two-stall stable in the Marstens' backyard where Phil's horse, Teddy, lived. But a year or two ago Phil's younger sister had gotten her first pony, so now A.J. boarded Crystal at Cross County, the stable where both boys had learned to ride.

"Phil should be able to find out what time A.J. usually goes over there to exercise her," she said logically. "Then I thought if we sort of ambushed him on his way out of the stable . . ."

"We could force him to talk to us," Alex finished for her. "Or at least to stick around and listen to us. Physically, if necessary."

Lisa gulped. She hadn't thought that far ahead. "I doubt physical force will be necessary," she said. "I mean, once he sees us there and realizes there's no easy escape, he's got to give up and hear us out. Right?"

"Probably," Alex agreed. "But desperate times call for desperate measures, right? So we'll be ready for anything."

Lisa nodded reluctantly. As much as she hated the thought of resorting to physical force, she had to admit that her boyfriend was right about things being desperate. And if it came down to it, it wouldn't be any problem at all for the guys to restrain A.J. long enough to make him listen to what they had to say. A.J. had always been slight, and he was still shorter than average—Phil could probably subdue him all on his own if necessary.

"We'll be ready for anything," she agreed softly.

The oven timer began chiming gently. "Garlic bread's ready," Alex announced, grabbing an oven mitt from its hook on the side of the refrigerator.

"Everything else is just about ready, too." Lisa glanced at her watch and switched off the burner under the pasta pot. "I wonder what's keeping Mom? Usually she can't get away from her miserable job fast enough. She's almost half an hour late. I hope her boss isn't making her—"

The phone's shrill ring interrupted her. Lisa hurried over and grabbed the receiver. "Hello?" she said.

"Lisa, honey," her mother's breathless voice came from the other end of the line. "It's me. I just realized the time, and I thought I should call so you didn't wait dinner for me."

"What?" Lisa's heart sank. If her mother's slimy boss was forcing her to stay late to do more inventory or something, that would surely mean the end of her refreshing good mood. "Why?"

Mrs. Atwood laughed. "Don't sound so heart-broken, sweetie," she teased lightly. "I'm sure you can manage without me for one night. I'm just going to grab a bite to eat with a friend from work."

Lisa was too surprised by that to answer for a moment. *Since when does Mom have friends at work?* she wondered. *I thought everyone except her loser boss was some kind of student. Besides, even if someone her own age started, she's not exactly a friend magnet these days.*

"Okay, then," her mother chirped. "I'll see you later tonight, sweetie."

"Bye, Mom." Lisa hung up and turned to face Alex, shaking her head in amazement. "I hope .

you're hungry. Mom's suddenly turned into a social butterfly. She won't be home for dinner."

Alex raised an eyebrow in surprise. "Wow," he said. "Call out the press."

"I know." Lisa walked over to turn down the stove burner. "I guess wonders never cease."

SIX

"**H**urry up," Stevie commanded. "It's six-oh-two."

Alex shot her a disgruntled look as he pulled a sweater over his head. "I know, I know," he said. "And a minute ago it was six-oh-one. I'm moving as fast as I can."

Stevie glanced at her watch again, feeling anxious. It was Friday, and they were due over at Cross County Stables by six-thirty to put Lisa's plan into action. Stevie wasn't sure it would work, but at this point she was willing to try just about anything. And Phil had actually sounded kind of hopeful about the whole thing when he'd called to set the time. "Come on," she said as her brother grabbed his sneakers out of the hall closet. "We're going to have to practically break the sound barrier as it is. We don't want to be late or A.J. could get away."

"It's bad enough I had to gulp down my dinner as fast as I could to be ready on time," Alex com-

79

plained, hopping on one foot as he pulled on his left sneaker. The Lakes' dog, a big golden retriever named Bear, wandered out of the living room, yawned, and gazed curiously at Alex as he lost his balance and crashed into the wall. "Do you expect me to go barefoot, too?"

Stevie ignored him. She knew he was grumpy because he hadn't had time for a third helping of mashed potatoes. Besides, her own stomach was feeling a little unsettled at the moment—she wasn't sure whether it was nerves or the result of eating too fast. Among his other new antisocial habits, A.J. had taken to going over to his stable when most people, including his own family, were eating dinner so that he wouldn't have to talk to anyone. That was fine with Stevie, even though it had meant bolting her own dinner. It meant there wouldn't be any interruptions.

And if the guys have to knock him down a few times to knock some sense into him, there won't be anyone to come rushing to his rescue, she thought grimly, leaning over to scratch Bear behind his furry butterscotch-colored ears. She knew that Lisa and Carole still felt a bit queasy at the idea that they might have to resort to physically restraining him to get A.J. to listen to them. But Stevie was well past that by now. She was ready for anything. She just wanted to resolve this—today.

That was one reason she'd made an extra effort to drum up more people for this confrontation than the last one—more friends from school, from Cross County, from Pine Hollow. Lisa and some of the others might think the purpose of the big crowd was to impress upon A.J. just how many people his behavior was affecting, and that was certainly part of it. But between themselves, Phil and Stevie were completely honest about the other benefit. The more people there were surrounding him, the easier it would be to intimidate him into listening to them.

"Anyway, I don't know why you're rushing me." Alex was still complaining as he grabbed the car keys off the hall table. "Lisa isn't even here yet, and neither is—"

The doorbell cut him off. "That's probably them now," Stevie announced, shoving Bear aside unceremoniously and grabbing the keys out of her brother's hand before he could react. She had no intention of letting him drive today. If she had to sit in the passenger's seat all the way to Cross County with nothing to do, she was liable to go crazy.

As Alex opened the door and met Lisa with a quick kiss, Stevie turned to grab her purse with her driver's license inside. As she did, she saw her younger brother, Michael, wander into the hall.

"Are you guys still here?" Michael said, checking his watch and ignoring Bear, who had wandered over and leaned amiably against his legs. "I thought you were all rushing off for your big A.J. thing."

"We're leaving," Stevie said shortly, noticing that Lisa had entered alone and shut the door behind her. That meant there was still one member of their party who hadn't arrived yet. "Just as soon as the last one of A.J.'s *real* friends gets here." She was feeling more than a little annoyed with Michael at the moment. She had hoped he would want to come along and be a part of things—he had known A.J. just as long as the rest of them, and the older boy had always been nice to him. But Michael had claimed to have other plans that evening. *As if a thirteen-year-old's plans could be so important!* Stevie thought irritably, turning away to greet Lisa.

"Are we ready to go?" Lisa asked, sounding slightly nervous.

"We will be," Alex replied. "As soon as— Aha!" he interrupted himself as the doorbell rang again.

"Since when does he ring the doorbell?" Stevie muttered as she flung the door open. "It's about time! We were waiting . . ."

Her voice trailed off as she saw who was standing there. It was a girl a few years younger than Stevie, petite and pixie-faced with long brown hair. Stevie vaguely recognized her as a neighbor who lived across the street from Lisa. What was her name again?

"Fawn," she managed, digging up the name from some corner of her memory. "Fawn Montgomery. Hi. What are you doing here?"

The younger girl's cheeks were pink. She glanced shyly at Stevie from beneath long lashes. "Um, hi," she said hesitantly. "Um, is Michael—"

"Hi!" Michael said, shoving his way past Stevie, his jacket in hand. "Sorry about that. I thought they'd be gone by now." He shot Stevie and Alex a dirty look. "Come on, let's go."

Stevie's jaw dropped as she took in his red face and embarrassed expression. She exchanged looks of amazement with her twin. So Michael had a little girlfriend! That explained a lot about his extra-weird behavior for the past week or so. . . .

But Stevie didn't have time to ponder that then. They were already late.

Lisa was staring toward the door as Michael slammed it behind him and Fawn. "Was that—"

"Yeah, yeah," Stevie said impatiently, opening the door and glancing toward the street, ignoring Michael and Fawn, who were hurrying off down the sidewalk. "Looks like Michael's joined the dating game."

"I wonder if Mom and Dad know?" Alex commented, shoving Bear back inside as he and Lisa followed Stevie onto the front porch. Mr. and Mrs. Lake were out at a business dinner.

"Worry about it later," Stevie said briskly. She had just spied another familiar figure climbing out of a battered old Volkswagen in front of the house. "Chad's here. At last."

"Chad's coming?" Lisa looked surprised. "Doesn't he have classes?"

Alex glanced up at her as he checked to make sure the door had locked behind them. "Not this late on Fridays," he replied. "He thought he could catch a ride down from school in time to come with us."

Stevie was already heading for the driveway as her older brother waved good-bye to the attractive girl behind the wheel and hurried toward the group. "Sorry I'm late," Chad called, running a hand through his sandy brown hair, which Stevie noticed had grown a little long since he'd left at the end of the summer. "We blew a tire on the way down, and—"

"Forget it," Stevie said, opening the door of the little blue car she and Alex shared. "Hop in. You can sit in the back since you were late."

Chad grinned at her. "Good to see you too, sis," he said as he managed to fold his lanky frame into the tiny backseat of the two-door car. "You know, I turned down a date with a hot fine arts major to come to this thing."

Stevie didn't bother to respond. Her older brother was legendary for switching girlfriends more often than most people changed their shirts.

She waved to Alex and Lisa, who were coming toward the car much too slowly for her taste, their hands intertwined. "Move it," she said. "It's already almost quarter after. We don't want to miss him."

Twenty minutes later, Stevie settled herself more comfortably on the grass behind the hedge that surrounded Cross County Stables' small, hard-packed dirt parking lot. From where she was sitting, she could see the handlebars of A.J.'s familiar green ten-speed through a bare spot in the hedge.

"I'm glad we didn't miss him," she told Phil for about the fourth time, glancing around at the crowd of almost two dozen people who had turned out. "If Alex and Lisa had their way, we'd still be back at that stop sign outside of town." She'd had to drive a little faster than she normally did to get there on time, and her passengers had seemed kind of frightened at moments—except for Chad, who had kept making jokes about the sound barrier and the speed of light from his spot in the backseat. As they had all climbed out of the car a couple of minutes earlier, Lisa had joked a bit shakily that she was never riding with Stevie again. In spite of their comments, Stevie knew that her friends were pleased to see her relaxed and confident behind the wheel—especially after the events of the summer. And after all, they were all there in one piece and on schedule, and that was what really mattered right then.

"I'm glad you guys are here." The petite redhead sitting on Phil's other side had just leaned over to address Stevie. "I'm so nervous I could die. I just hope this does some good."

"Don't worry, Julianna." Stevie smiled at A.J.'s ex-girlfriend. "I'm sure it will. It's got to."

"I think one of the hardest things will be leaving PC," Emily said thoughtfully, picking at a blade of grass.

Lisa pretended to be insulted. "PC?" she said, leaning back on her elbows as she waited with the others for A.J. to emerge from the stable. "Hey, what about the rest of us? Aren't you going to miss us, too?"

"Sure," Emily agreed with a grin. "But remember, PC can't use e-mail." She shrugged. "He tried, but it was no good. His hooves are just too big for the keys."

Lisa laughed. "Well, e-mail or no e-mail, we're all going to miss you like crazy." She automatically glanced at Stevie and Carole as she said it. Stevie was sitting nearby with Phil and Julianna. Carole was leaning against a tree a few yards beyond them, talking to Ben.

"You'll have to promise to send me pictures of Prancer's foals after they're born," Emily told Lisa. "Do you know how to do that by e-mail?"

"I'll figure it out," Lisa assured her. She was dying to tell Emily the other part of the Prancer secret. But a promise was a promise. Telling Alex was one thing—that was sort of like telling another part of herself. But Carole would never forgive her if she told anyone else, even Emily. "You'll have to figure it out, too—we'll definitely want to see pictures of your new house and all your new Australian friends, and of course your new horse."

"It's going to be pretty scary at first," Emily said thoughtfully. "Getting used to all that new stuff, I mean. But I think I'm mostly looking forward to it. Does that seem weird?"

Lisa shrugged. Maybe coming from some people it would have seemed kind of odd—most people weren't that eager to start all over in a new place. But Emily had always been one of the bravest and most adventurous people Lisa knew. "Not really," she said. "I think you'll do great." She sighed, thinking about how much she'd miss Emily's familiar cheerful, high-spirited presence. "I

just hope the rest of us can survive without you."
Suddenly she brightened. "Hey, I just had a great
idea. Why don't we throw you a big good-bye
blowout party before you go?"

"Why don't you?" Emily agreed quickly with a
wide, surprised grin. "You'll have to hurry,
though. We're shipping out the week before Halloween."

That didn't give them much time. Lisa was already wondering what she'd gotten herself into by
suggesting a big bash. Still, Emily definitely deserved a party. And if everything worked the way
it was supposed to today, maybe they'd have even
more to celebrate.

"Don't worry," she told Emily. "I'll talk to
Stevie and Alex about it as soon as this A.J. thing
is over. If anyone can plan a party to remember in
record time, it's the two of them."

". . . and so I told Max I thought Samson and
I should enter Open Jumping as well as maybe
some Intermediate and Junior classes," Carole said
eagerly. She glanced automatically toward the
Cross County stable building. The whole group
had been waiting for a good ten minutes, but
there was still no sign of A.J., which meant that
Carole had some more time to talk over her
Colesford entries with Ben. She was still a little
surprised that Ben had wanted to tag along with

her to this meeting—he hardly knew A.J.—but she wasn't going to worry about it. It was his business if he wanted to spend his evening standing around in the grass beside an almost empty parking lot, not hers. Her thoughts returned to the horse show. "I mean, I know a lot of the riders there will have a lot more experience at these kinds of shows than I do, but I figure that with Samson's talent we should be able to hold our own at least."

"Hmmm," Ben said.

Carole took that as an invitation to continue, so she did. "Even if we don't win anything at this show—and you never know, we could surprise everyone, right?—it should give me a really good idea of Samson's strengths and weaknesses in competition. That way I'll have a better idea about what I should be working on in his training, and then the next show we enter—"

"Carole." Ben's voice held a slight edge as he interrupted her stream of words.

She stared at him in surprise. "What?" she asked, a bit irritated that he didn't seem to be paying attention to her plans for Samson after all. Wasn't he interested in hearing about Pine Hollow's newest star? He certainly didn't look very interested. Usually the one time he relaxed a little was when he was discussing Pine Hollow's residents with her or Max. Now he seemed anything but relaxed. His brow was furrowed beneath the shock of dark hair that hung over his forehead, and he was standing so far back toward the hedge that he was in danger of falling into it.

"I just don't think . . ." Ben paused and took a deep breath. His dark eyes danced here and there, seemingly looking everywhere except directly at her. "Be careful."

"Of course I'll be careful," Carole said quickly. "Do you think I've never been in a horse show before? I really don't think Open Jumping will be dangerous for Samson, not when he's clearly—"

"No." Ben's voice was louder when he cut her off this time. "Don't get so caught up with that horse."

Carole wasn't sure how to respond. What was Ben driving at? Was this about her work at the stable? Was he jealous that Max had assigned her an interesting task like training Samson?

That couldn't be it. Ben had as many training duties as she did. It wasn't as though he was spending all his time mucking out stalls while she was off practicing her jumping. Then what? Did this have something to do with their friendship?

"I—I don't understand," she said uncertainly.

Ben shrugged and shoved his hands in his jeans pockets. "He's not the only horse around."

"What do you—" Unbidden, an image of Starlight flashed into her mind. Carole gulped and started again. "What do you mean by that? I know he's not the only horse around. He just happens to be the horse Max asked me to work with the most these days. You know that."

Ben took a deep breath. "Samson's taking up a lot of your time . . ."

His voice trailed off. Carole could feel anger bubbling up inside her. Where did Ben get off lecturing her on time management, anyway? He was the one who'd practically stopped speaking to her that summer when she'd tried to find out more about him. He was the one who valued his precious privacy so much he seemed willing to go through life without any real friends. Carole had tried to be a friend to him despite that, and look where it had gotten her. "I can take care of my own schedule, Ben," she said coldly.

"Sure," he said, meeting her gaze at last.

When she saw the look of concern in his dark eyes, Carole was a little taken aback. It was almost as if he knew about . . . But no. She hadn't told anyone about that test—not her father, not her best friends, and certainly not Ben Marlow. If any of them ever found out what she'd done, they would probably never be able to look at her the same way again. *Anyway, my problems at school don't have anything to do with my work at the stable,* she told herself firmly, doing her best to ignore the tight little knot that seemed to cinch her stomach these days anytime she thought about that test. *And that means it's none of Ben's business.*

Ben was watching her closely, and the doubt in his eyes was still obvious.

That brought Carole's irritation sweeping back. He wasn't her father or her boss. He wasn't even much of a friend most of the time. It wasn't as if she could ever count on any answers from him.

"Well, whatever *you* may think," she said evenly, glaring at him, "I guess Max must not agree with you. If he thought I was having some kind of problem, he never would have asked me to ride at Colesford."

That thought made her feel better immediately. Max was the one who had asked her to train Samson. He was the one who'd invited her to ride Samson in the big show. Who was Ben to second-guess those decisions? And why was she even standing there listening to him?

"Look," she said abruptly. "If you've got a problem with me or my work, you'll just have to deal with it yourself."

"But I just want to—"

Carole didn't let him finish. "Because as far as I'm concerned," she snapped, "everything's just fine." With that, she hurried off toward Lisa and Emily without a backward glance.

Stevie checked her watch. It had stopped sometime during the ride between her house and Cross County Stables, so she grabbed Phil's wrist and checked his. A.J. still hadn't showed, though a few minutes ago someone—a boy from Cross County High School Stevie didn't know—had sneaked over to check the stable and reported that A.J. was definitely still inside.

Stevie sighed impatiently. A couple of other Cross County students had come over and started talking to Phil and Julianna about some sort of history project, and Stevie wasn't interested. Glancing around, she saw Alex and Chad standing near a break in the hedge a few yards away.

"Be right back," she told Phil absently, already climbing to her feet.

She hurried over to join her two brothers. "Hey, Stevie." Chad glanced at her. "Is A.J. coming?"

"Not yet." She glanced over her shoulder toward the stable roof, which was barely visible above the line of the hedge. "I hope he comes out soon. The suspense is killing me."

Alex grinned. "So what did you think of Michael's little surprise visitor?"

"Oh!" Stevie was genuinely amazed to find that she'd almost forgotten about the Fawn incident already. But now that she remembered, she started grinning, too. Michael hadn't even been interested in girls the last time Stevie had checked, and now here he was with a real live girlfriend. . . . "I think it's very interesting," she told her brothers with a smirk. "In fact, it's so interesting that I may have to find a way to express my great interest to Michael."

Chad looked slightly worried. "What do you mean?" he asked cautiously. "You know Michael's kind of touchy these days. I'm not sure he's going to be in the mood for any teasing about something like this."

Stevie shrugged and shot her older brother an annoyed glance. "Since when are you Mr. Sensitive? Anyway, this will just be payback for all the teasing I got from him—from all three of you— back when Phil and I first started going out." She wrinkled her nose as she thought of those days. "If Michael can dish it out, he'll have to take it."

"Aren't you getting a little too old for that revenge stuff?" Alex commented.

"Watch it, buddy, or you'll be next." Stevie shot him a wicked grin. "Remember, I have really easy access to *your* girlfriend. And I'm not afraid to use it." She rubbed her palms together briskly, already thinking and planning. "Let's see," she said pensively. "Michael was always a sucker for phone pranks. I could call and pretend to be Fawn and then record all his embarrassing lovey-dovey chat to play over the PA system at school. And then there's her name, of course. *Fawn, Fawn*—I should be able to do something with that. Maybe I should rent *Bambi* and see if it inspires anything. . . ."

As she leaned against a tree on the grass near the Cross County parking lot, Callie found her gaze wandering toward Emily for the fifth time in as many minutes. She sighed and forced her attention back to George Wheeler, who was talking earnestly at her about some assignment they were supposed to do that weekend for their chemistry class.

"I'm sorry," she told him. "What did you just say?"

George looked a bit hurt. "I said if you want, we could get together at the library or someplace and go over that lab," he said. "I mean, since you said you were having trouble with it today in class."

"Oh, right." Callie smiled apologetically at him. George might be a little serious and bland for her taste, but he was a nice enough guy. If he weren't, he wouldn't have given up his evening to sit there and wait around for A.J., who was a casual acquaintance at best. More importantly, George was a whiz in chemistry, while Callie herself was definitely not. "Sorry. I guess I'm preoccupied by all the suspense about A.J."

That was a white lie, since Callie had hardly thought about A.J. since she and Scott had arrived at the designated meeting place. After all, there wasn't really much to think about—they had all been over the problem often enough in the past few weeks. All they could do now was wait for him to show up and take it from there.

"Oh," George said, not seeming to suspect a thing. "That's okay, I understand. I mean, I don't know A.J. that well myself, but . . ."

Suddenly feeling guilty for fibbing to someone as trusting as George, Callie cut him off. "Actually," she said, "that's not really why I was distracted." She took a deep breath. "You see, I just found out that Emily—you know Emily, right?—is moving to Australia in, like, two weeks."

George nodded and glanced toward Emily, who was talking to Lisa and Carole nearby. "I heard about that. It must be kind of a shock—I mean, she's been helping you with—you know—your leg and everything. Her horse, too. Right?"

"Exactly." Callie smiled with relief at not having to spell it out for him. George was clearly a little uncomfortable pointing out her temporary handicap, and she hurried to put him at ease. "So you can understand why the news took me by surprise."

George nodded quickly. "You're being awfully brave about it." His deep-set gray eyes gazed into hers sincerely. "In fact, I—I've been wanting to tell you, I think you've been really brave about this whole thing. The accident, I mean, and—well, you know."

"Thanks, George. That's sweet of you to say." Callie was feeling a little uncomfortable with this conversation herself. After what had happened with that newspaper article, it was harder than ever to have an honest conversation and talk about her feelings. Still, she was glad she'd told George the truth. He really was a nice person—and Callie could use as many kind, caring, trustworthy friends as she could get. She smiled at him. "Anyway, your idea about getting together this weekend sounds good." She glanced at her brother, who was sprawled on the grass nearby chatting with a couple of Cross County kids. "I'll just have to check and see when Scott can drive me."

George nodded. "Great!"

"Hello, everyone," a breezy voice announced from the break in the hedge. "Hope I'm not late for the party."

Callie looked up in surprise as Veronica di-Angelo stepped through the hedge and glanced around at the group, a self-satisfied little smirk on her face. "Uh-oh," Callie murmured under her breath. She couldn't believe Veronica had actually showed up. Why would she bother? She didn't care about A.J.—or anyone else but herself, for that matter. Callie had seen enough of her in the past week to realize that. Veronica had sought her out at every opportunity, stopping her in the halls between classes, waving at her during morning assemblies, even inviting Callie to join her at lunch. Callie had managed to fend off most of her advances politely enough, but she should have known that Veronica wouldn't give up that easily, not when she'd obviously made up her mind that Callie was socially important. Now it seemed she was even willing to pursue Callie outside of school. . . .

At that moment Veronica's roving eye landed on Scott. Her smile growing wider and more self-satisfied than ever, she made a beeline for him, lowering herself carefully to the ground by his side. "Hi there," she said loudly enough for the entire group to hear. "Is this seat taken?"

SEVEN

S tevie blinked. "Somebody pinch me," she commented, "because this has to be a nightmare."

Alex obligingly reached over and pinched her hard on the arm.

"Ow!" Stevie glared and punched him, then rubbed her arm as her gaze returned to Veronica, who was chatting animatedly at Scott. He was smiling back at her amiably. "What's she doing here? Can't she flirt with Scott on her own time?"

Chad was staring at Veronica. "Is that who I think it is?" He sounded a bit awestruck. "Boy, did she fill out nicely. I mean, she was cute even back when I saw her last, but now—"

Stevie smacked him on the shoulder. "Cut the drooling, dork," she said irritably. "You should know better. Veronica's a troll, no matter what she looks like. Even Callie sees that, though of course you know her—she always has to be polite, so she . . ."

Her voice trailed off as she suddenly realized who must have mentioned this gathering to Veronica. She turned and hurried over to Callie, who was sitting on the grass with George.

Callie gave her a sheepish smile. "Hi, Stevie," she said. "Did I forget to mention that I told Veronica about what we were doing?"

Stevie crossed her arms over her chest and waited.

"She dragged it out of me," Callie explained. "She was bugging me all week to go shopping with her today—I had to give her an excuse. I thought this would be the one thing she'd never want to be part of."

"Hmmm." Stevie's gaze wandered toward Veronica, who was leaning closer to Scott, whispering something into his ear and smiling. She couldn't help noticing that Scott was still smiling, too. She rolled her eyes. "Well, I guess you've got more sense than your brother, anyway. He actually looks happy that she's here."

"He looks that way with everyone, remember?" Callie said. "It's one of those little politicians' tricks he's picked up from Dad over the years."

"Right." Stevie was about to go on, but at that moment there was a flash of movement on the other side of the hedge. A second later, the Cross County boy who'd been acting as lookout raced through the break.

"He's coming!" he announced breathlessly. "He just left the building, and he's heading this way."

Immediately Stevie was all action. "Everybody quiet," she commanded. "Gather over here near the opening in the hedge. Phil's going to lure him back here, and then I want everyone to surround him." She glanced around to be sure she had everyone's undivided attention, feeling a little like a general planning strategy in a key battle. "Don't let him out of the circle until we get some answers. Understood?"

There were nods all around as people scurried to get into position. Stevie herself took up a post near the break in the hedge. Without speaking, Alex and Phil took up positions on either side of her. Stevie smiled grimly, certain that they were thinking the same thing she was: If A.J. wanted to escape this time, he was going to have to get past them first.

Phil leaned over and peered through the break. "Here goes nothing," he whispered. He darted out into the parking lot.

Stevie held her breath. Was this going to work?

A moment later Phil's voice drifted toward them from the other side of the hedge. "Hey, man," he said cheerfully, sounding surprised. "What are you doing here?"

Stevie grinned, feeling proud of him. If his planned career as a lawyer didn't work out, there was a fine future for him in acting.

A.J.'s voice was quieter. "Phil?" he said, not sounding half as pleased to see Phil as Phil had sounded to see him. "I'm here checking on Crystal. What are *you* doing here?"

Phil mumbled something that Stevie couldn't hear. Then he went on. "But actually, now that we're both here, I wanted to talk to you about something."

"I'm kind of in a hurry. . . ." A.J.'s voice was taking on that cold, sullen tone it had started slipping into lately.

"This won't take long."

A moment later there was a cry of annoyance and a rustle of shrubbery, and Phil popped through the break in the hedge holding A.J. firmly by the arm. The smaller guy was squirming to break free, protesting all the while.

But he stopped when he saw the others. "What's going on here?" he demanded.

Phil dropped his arm, stepping back to take his place in the circle. Stevie and Alex had already moved to close off A.J.'s access to the opening in the hedge. "We just want to talk to you, A.J.," he said calmly.

A.J. glared at the circle of his friends. He

looked angry and defiant and upset and a bit frightened, like a caged animal deciding whether to choose fight or flight. *Good,* Stevie thought, forcing down the feelings of pity welling up as A.J.'s gaze met hers for a moment and then bounced away. *He's more likely to talk if he's scared.*

"I don't know what you people are up to," A.J. said after a moment, anger seeming to take the upper hand. "But I don't want any part of it. I'm out of here."

He started toward the break in the hedge, but Alex took a step forward and shook his head. "Sorry, A.J." he said, his voice firm. "We'd really like you to stick around for a little while."

A.J. hesitated, seeming confused. "I've got to go," he insisted. He took a couple more steps toward the break. "Let me go, all right?"

Stevie moved closer to her twin's side. "No way, A.J. Not until you hear what we have to say. We've been patient long enough."

Finally A.J. seemed to realize that they weren't going to let him through. He scowled, glancing around as if searching for a weak link. But then his shoulders slumped and he shrugged resignedly. "Whatever," he said heavily. "Why don't you just say your piece, then. But hurry up—I haven't eaten yet and I'm hungry."

"Fine." Phil was obviously struggling to control

his temper, and Stevie shot him a sympathetic glance.

Remember that we're here to help A.J., she thought, willing her message to reach Phil somehow and keep him calm. *Blowing up won't help anyone.*

"We're all here because we feel like we don't know you anymore," Phil went on evenly, his gaze never leaving A.J.'s face. "You've completely changed, and everyone's wondering why."

"We're your friends, A.J.," Julianna put in, her voice soft and pleading. "We want to help you. You can trust us." A few of the others murmured or nodded their agreement.

A.J. just shrugged. "Nothing's wrong."

"How can you say that?" Stevie protested. "You've been moping around for weeks, skipping school, refusing to talk to the people who care about you. . . ."

"It's nothing," A.J. said sullenly. "There's nothing I want to talk about."

"A.J." Phil took a step toward his friend. "Please. Just tell us what's bothering you."

"Nothing," A.J. said again. "None of your business."

Stevie clenched her fists at her sides, wondering why she'd ever thought this would work. The way things were looking, they could keep A.J. there for days and he still wouldn't tell them anything.

Suddenly Veronica stepped forward. "Listen, A.J.," she said briskly. "We all have better things to do than hang around here while you don't tell us what's turning you into such a freak." She tossed her head. "Besides, we all know what the problem is, even if you won't admit it."

Stevie's jaw dropped. She had almost forgotten that Veronica was there—all she'd done since she arrived was hang on Scott's arm and bat her eyelashes at him. Stevie would have bet money that Veronica didn't even remember the reason they were all supposed to be there. So what was she doing?

Everyone else, including A.J., seemed too stunned to react as well. Veronica put her hands on her hips and stared at A.J. "Everyone else here is just too timid to say what we're all thinking," she went on bluntly. "We all know what causes people to change like this, to get weird and antisocial like you're acting right now."

A.J. looked startled. "What do you mean?"

Veronica rolled her eyes. "Drugs, of course," she said disdainfully. "And I know we've never been that close or anything, A.J., but I just have to tell you: Messing around with that stuff is way dangerous—not to mention stupid and totally uncool."

"Drugs?" A.J. blurted out. "You think this has

something to do with drugs?" He let out a short, disbelieving laugh. He turned away from Veronica and stared at Phil. "I've never touched a drug in my life. I don't even drink at parties. Don't you know me better than that?"

Phil knew an opening when he saw one. "I thought I did, man," he said sharply. "But what else are we supposed to think?"

A.J. shook his head vigorously. "It's not drugs."

"What then?" Stevie had run out of patience. Veronica's tactless accusation had actually done the trick—it had broken through A.J.'s defenses and gotten him talking. She wasn't about to waste the opportunity. "What is it, if it's not drugs? Is it gambling? Did you run someone down with your bike?"

"What about medical problems?" Alex put in. "Do you have a disease or a tumor or something?"

"Or school trouble?" Lisa added. "Are you flunking out? Having trouble? A learning problem, maybe?"

"Is one of the teachers hassling you?" a girl Stevie didn't know suggested. "Mr. Hall can be a real jerk, and I know you have his class."

Carole gasped. "It's not Crystal, is it?" She glanced toward the stable. "Is she sick?"

Veronica was shaking her head through all this. "You guys are way off," she announced. "It's definitely got to be drugs. Or maybe drinking. He could be an alcoholic." She turned to A.J. curiously. "Is there any history of that sort of thing in your family? I heard it can be, like, genetic."

"It's not about me, is it?" Julianna's voice was soft but steady. "Does this have something to do with us?"

A.J. took a step backward, looking a bit overwhelmed by the sudden onslaught. He held up his hands helplessly. "It's not you," he told Julianna. He glanced around at the others. "It's not any of the things you think. I told you, it's nothing."

Something inside Stevie finally snapped. She couldn't stand to hear him say that one more time, not now when she thought they'd finally broken through. "Don't lie to us!" she shouted, taking a step forward. "Don't you dare lie to us about this anymore, A.J. We're sick of it!" She shook off Phil's restraining hand on her arm and stepped forward again until she was staring directly into A.J.'s face. This mystery couldn't go on any longer. She couldn't stand it. Not for one more day, not for one more minute. "There's something going on with you, and we want to know what it is! Now!"

"Forget it, Stevie," Veronica said blandly from across the circle. "When someone's into drugs, they don't care about anything or anyone else."

"That's true," someone else agreed.

A.J. took a step back, looking more overwhelmed than ever by Stevie's outburst. He glanced at Veronica. "I told you, it's not—" He backed away another step and stared around at the group. "I'm not—I mean, why can't you just—"

"Why can't you just tell us the *truth*!" Stevie shrieked, startling even herself with the force of her voice. She stepped forward again and jammed one finger at A.J.'s chest, shoving him back another step. "Just tell us! Tell us!"

"I *can't*!" A.J. cried, looking downright frightened this time. He held up his hands in an ineffectual attempt to keep Stevie away from him. "It's too . . . I just can't."

"You have to, man," Phil said, his voice as steely as Stevie had ever heard it. "This has gone far enough."

"I told you!" Veronica whined loudly. "It's no use talking to him. He's probably strung out on something right now. You should just call some drug hotline or something and let them handle it."

"Stop it!" A.J. squeezed his eyes shut and slapped his hands over his ears. "Why aren't you listening to me? I already told you this has nothing to do with drugs or anything like that. Why can't you just leave me alone?"

"Because we're your friends," Phil said calmly.

"We're never going to leave you alone until you talk to us."

"*Never,*" Stevie snapped, jabbing him in the chest one more time.

A.J.'s eyes flew open and he slapped her hand away. "Fine!" he snapped back. "If you want to know so badly, why don't you talk to my parents? Maybe they'll tell you, even though they never bothered to tell me."

"Tell you what?" Stevie asked, confused.

Behind her, she heard Veronica gasp. "You mean your parents are the ones who got you started? Are they junkies, too?"

A.J. ignored her. He was staring at the ground now, his expression weary and somehow defeated. "They never bothered to say a word," he murmured, more to himself than to anyone else.

Stevie opened her mouth, but Phil nudged her in the ribs. "You mean this is a family thing?" he asked A.J. gently. "Do you want to go somewhere and talk about it—just the two of us? We can do that."

A.J. shrugged, and Stevie saw that his eyes were shining with held-back tears. "Forget it," he said. "I didn't want anyone to know. It's too . . . But if you're all going to start telling people I'm a drug addict . . . I don't . . . Maybe I should just . . ." The struggle going on within him was evident on his face, which shifted rapidly from one tortured expression to another. There was a moment of breathless silence as everyone waited for him to go on. When he spoke again, still staring at the ground, his voice was little more than a whisper. "I found out that I'm not—that I'm— I'm adopted."

EIGHT

Lisa was as stunned as everyone else by A.J.'s revelation.

Adopted? she thought in disbelief, thinking of A.J.'s father's auburn hair, which so closely matched his son's—his *adopted* son's, she corrected herself. *No wonder A.J. was so freaked when he found out,* she thought.

But there was no time at the moment to ponder the ironies of the universe. After a second or two of shocked silence, everyone had started talking at once—to A.J., to each other, and, in Veronica's case, to herself.

"I thought it was drugs!" she exclaimed, throwing up her hands and sounding oddly disappointed. "I still think it's drugs."

Lisa glanced at A.J. His eyes were starting to look as red as his hair, and he once again seemed to be looking for an escape route. This time Lisa thought he should find one. Now that his secret was out, there was no reason he should be completely humiliated in front of all his friends.

She nudged Alex and Scott, who were standing on either side of her. "Open up," she whispered. She stepped back a few paces. The guys did the same.

A.J. spotted his opportunity and took it, racing for the hole in the circle and then the break in the hedge. As he passed her, Lisa would have sworn he shot her a grateful look.

"Hey!" Stevie shouted as A.J. disappeared. "Where are you going?"

But it was too late. Seconds later, the sound of bicycle tires skidding on dirt answered her question.

"I think he needs to be alone right now," Lisa said.

Stevie gave her an irritated glance. "Did you let him go?" she said. "How come? We were just getting through to him. Besides, he barely told us anything."

Phil put a soothing hand on her arm. "He told us enough," he said, his face pale but calm. "I think it's safe to say that our plan worked this time."

"Right," Lisa agreed, slipping her hand into Alex's. "Our job here is done. He doesn't need a crowd now."

A few other people nodded. "Maybe someone

ought to follow him, though," someone suggested. "Make sure he's okay."

"Phil?" Scott suggested. "You'd be the logical choice—you've known him longer than anyone here."

Phil nodded. "I'm on it." He glanced at Stevie. "Okay?"

"Okay," she said reluctantly.

Lisa smiled in relief. "This turned out better than I expected," she told Alex quietly as Phil departed and other people started breaking into smaller groups or drifting toward the parking lot. "I'm just glad A.J.'s not mixed up with drugs."

"Me too." Alex squeezed her hand comfortingly. "And I'm sure he'll feel better once he and Phil have talked."

"I hope so." Lisa tried to imagine how A.J. must have felt when he'd discovered he was adopted. Would it be easier or harder than what she had gone through when her father had walked out? Lisa had no idea, but she was sure it couldn't have been much fun either way. "I wonder how he found out, anyway?" she mused as she and Alex strolled slowly toward Stevie and Chad, who were talking with Julianna and a couple of the other Cross County kids. "He said his parents didn't tell him."

Alex shrugged. "I guess Phil will ask him," he

said. "I'm sure we'll all know everything there is to know soon enough."

Carole had been so distracted by the events around her that, for a few minutes at least, she had all but forgotten Ben's annoying comments. But once A.J. and Phil had gone, their conversation crept back to the front of her mind.

She fingered her car keys in her jacket pocket. *I wish Ben hadn't decided to come today,* she thought petulantly. *Or at least I wish I hadn't been the one to give him a ride.* She didn't much feel like sharing an awkward twenty-minute car ride back to Pine Hollow.

Still, she didn't have much choice. She sighed, wondering idly what it would be like to be as selfish and fickle as Veronica, who probably wouldn't think twice about ditching someone without a ride if she was annoyed with him.

But I'm not like that, Carole thought. *Oh well. Might as well get it over with.*

Still feeling reluctant, she approached Ben, who was standing by himself near the break in the hedge. "Ready to go?" she asked, sounding as natural as she could. It wasn't easy, especially when she imagined she could still see all kinds of questions and accusations in Ben's dark eyes.

But he didn't speak. He just nodded and started walking toward her car.

Carole gritted her teeth and followed. Why did she let him get to her like this, anyway? *I can't help it,* she told herself. *He's just so—so aggravating sometimes.*

Ten minutes later, Callie managed to drag her brother away from a couple of guys from Cross County and a tedious conversation about politics. "Come on," she told him wearily. "Let's get going, okay?"

"Nice guys." Scott watched as his new friends wandered away toward their own car. "Interesting opinions."

"Whatever." Callie was used to Scott's inordinately social ways, but today they were wearing on her nerves. It had been a long day—not just because of what had happened with A.J., which had been draining enough. Callie had also been forced to endure another whole day of stares and whispers and too-friendly greetings from her schoolmates. She'd been through this sort of thing before and knew that the other students would get tired of talking about her family soon. But not soon enough for her. She wished she could be more like Scott, who could ignore the stares—at least in public. Sometimes, though, she wondered if he was really as unmoved by all the attention as he appeared.

As Scott dug into his pocket for his keys, Veronica came hurrying over. "There you are!" she exclaimed dramatically. "I'm so glad you haven't left yet."

Callie rolled her eyes. Hardly anyone had left yet. Despite the early moves toward getting in their cars, most of the people who had come to help were still hanging around, talking about what had happened—or maybe just talking. As far as Callie could tell, the only people who'd left so far besides A.J. and Phil were Carole and Ben.

"Still here," Scott told Veronica cheerfully. "What can I do for you, my friend?"

Veronica tilted her head to one side and smiled up at Scott beseechingly. "My car won't start."

"Do you want me to take a look?" Scott offered. "I'm not much of a mechanic, but I—"

"That's okay." Veronica put a hand on his elbow. "It's been acting up all week—I can call my mechanic to come tow it later. I was just hoping you could give me a ride back to Willow Creek."

Callie glanced at Veronica's sleek black sports car, which looked perfectly fine to her. She seriously doubted there was anything wrong with it.

If Scott suspected anything, he wasn't letting on. "Sure thing," he told Veronica graciously. "Your house is right on our way."

"Uh, excuse me."

Callie, Scott, and Veronica turned and saw George Wheeler standing behind them. He was scratching at his chin with one hand, an embarrassed expression on his round face. "Hey, George," Scott said easily. "What's up?"

"I—um, Carole gave me a ride over here," George said, looking more sheepish than ever. "From Pine Hollow. She was supposed to drive me back there when this was over, but I guess I was talking to someone and she must have, uh . . ."

Callie couldn't help smiling as she realized what George was trying to tell them. Scatterbrained Carole had struck again. She must have forgotten all about poor George, leaving him stranded miles from home without a ride. "Wow," she said. "That's pretty bad, even for Carole." She smiled sympathetically at George. "Don't take it personally. She could forget her own father if she got distracted talking about horses." She shook her head, amazed as she often was that Carole could be so absentminded and still manage to survive day-to-day life.

Scott clapped George on the shoulder. "Don't worry," he told him. "We were just about to head out. You're welcome to hitch a ride with us."

Carole clenched the steering wheel tightly in both hands, being careful to keep her eyes trained on the road in front of her. *I won't look over at him,* she told herself fiercely. *I won't let him think*

I care if he never says another word to me as long as we live.

Ben hadn't spoken at all since they'd left Cross County ten minutes earlier. He had just sat there, hunched over in the passenger seat, staring gloomily out the side window.

Carole was driving a little too fast, trying to get back to Pine Hollow and end this horribly awkward ride as soon as possible. Her foot pressed down a little harder on the gas pedal as she stared fixedly at the paved road surface in front of her, willing herself not to glance Ben's way.

"Carole?" His voice sounded worried.

"What?" she asked, triumph flooding through her. She had done it. She'd made him break the silence first!

"You're going to miss the turn."

She gasped and spun the wheel hard to the left, hitting the brakes at the same time. The car's tires squealed in protest as it spun and skidded to the side, and Ben gulped audibly as the car in the oncoming lane blared its horn at them. Carole squeezed her eyes shut and hit the gas again. The car jolted forward awkwardly, finally landing safe and sound in the correct lane of the side road before conking out completely.

"Oops," she said after a moment.

Ben didn't respond. He just glanced at her as she carefully started the car again. Soon they were driving down the side road at a much more sedate pace.

"Sorry about that," Carole said as soon as she felt she could trust her own voice again. "Um, I guess I was distracted."

Ben stayed silent for another long moment before speaking. "You've been distracted a lot lately," he said quietly. "Um, that's why I tried to say something earlier. You and Samson—"

"Me and Samson are just fine," Carole said sharply. "I mean Samson and I. We're fine and dandy. I told you that before. Why don't you listen?"

Ben scowled. "Odd question for you to ask," he snapped.

"What are you talking about?" Carole asked, stung by his cold, brusque tone.

"Nothing." With that, Ben fell silent again.

Carole wasn't about to argue anymore. "Fine." For the rest of the ride back to the stable, neither of them said another word.

Callie was feeling decidedly uncomfortable. Veronica had commandeered the front seat of Scott's car, which meant that Callie and George were crowded together in the cramped backseat. Normally that wouldn't have been such a bad thing—Callie's leg made getting in and out of the back of the car a little difficult, but not impossible. And sitting in the back had the advantage of making conversation with those in the front seat harder, and Callie certainly had no interest in making small talk with Veronica. But at the moment, the way George was looking at her, his eyes never wavering from her face, was making her think that maybe she had been missing something here. Did George think of her the way she thought of him—as a Pine Hollow pal, a chemistry crony? Or could she have totally missed the fact that he might be interested in something more?

Callie gazed out the window at the scenery speeding by along the two-lane highway that linked Cross County and Willow Creek. The trees were just starting to show their autumn colors, but Callie barely registered their beauty. She was busy sorting out this George business in her mind. Now that she thought about it, he had made a point of seeking her out earlier in the afternoon. And he had a way of turning up rather frequently when she was at the stable. When he mentioned that weekend's study date for the fourth time in ten minutes, Callie had to admit that she might be in trouble.

What have I gotten myself into? she wondered desperately as she did her best to keep smiling and nodding at whatever George said. *Why can't guys ever want to just be friends? I was looking for a study partner, not a date.*

The sudden shrill squeal of Veronica's laughter made her wince. Callie had been doing her best not to pay attention to what was going on in the front seat, but she'd overheard enough to realize that Veronica was coyly trying to get Scott to ask her out. He was more than a match for her wiles, though, deflecting every hint with an affable joke or witty comment. Callie idly wondered if he intended to blow her off completely and was trying to be tactful about it, or if he was just toying with her a little before he gave in and asked her. She certainly fit his type well enough—good-looking, self-confident, and definitely interested in him.

At least if she starts dating Scott, she might be too busy to keep after me to be her best friend, Callie thought, trying to look on the bright side.

"I was thinking," George said, breaking into her thoughts, "after we finish going over that lab, maybe we could stop by that little ice cream place in the shopping center, you know—*ulp.*"

Callie glanced at him. For the first time she noticed that his face had taken on a decidedly greenish tinge. He was clutching the side armrest so hard that his knuckles were dead white. "Are you okay?" she asked, relieved to have a reprieve from responding to his invitation. "You look a little sick."

George swallowed hard before answering. "It's just—um—I sometimes get kind of carsick.

"O-Only when I ride in the backseat, though." He looked sheepish.

"Why didn't you say so?" Callie leaned forward, truly alarmed by now at his queasy expression. She poked her brother's shoulder. "Pull over."

"What's wrong?" Scott was already steering the car toward the side of the road as he glanced back at her.

"George is carsick," Callie announced. "He needs to sit in the front seat."

"Whoa." Scott brought the car to a quick halt. "Sorry about that, buddy. You should have said something. I'm sure Veronica won't mind switching now, though."

"Right," Veronica said a bit sourly. She sighed heavily as she unhooked her seat belt and opened her door. "Whatever."

Callie rolled her eyes as Veronica stepped away from the car and crossed her arms over her chest, not bothering to help George climb out of the backseat of the two-door sports car, even when he almost tripped over the dangling seat belt.

Callie winced on his behalf. She hadn't bothered to really examine George as a guy before. All she'd needed to know up to this point was that he was an excellent rider and smart about chemistry. Now that she really checked him out, though, she found herself shaking her head involuntarily. He was so awkward, so nervous and nerdy. . . . How could he think she'd be interested in someone like him as more than a friend?

She immediately chastised herself for the uncharitable thought. *If I don't watch out, I'm going to start sounding like Veronica,* she scolded herself. *And after all, I'm not exactly a grand prize myself at the moment.* She glanced at her ugly metal crutches, which were propped beside her.

Still, she knew there was no way she could ever be interested in someone like George. He just wasn't her type. He was too safe, too dull and easy to read. She preferred guys who had a bit of an edge to them—something unexpected, mysterious, even dangerous.

She sighed as Veronica clambered into the backseat and plopped herself down, still looking annoyed. Soon George was settled in the front seat and Scott was pulling onto the road again.

Veronica pouted silently for a minute or two, then turned to Callie with a smile that looked a bit forced. "So," she said brightly. "I heard you're an endurance rider, Callie. That must be fun. I went on an endurance ride or two back when I was still riding a lot. Did you know I used to ride at Pine Hollow?"

Callie nodded, resigning herself to more pointless chitchat. She wondered if Veronica was really still interested in being friends with her or if she just wanted to use her to get to Scott. Either way, she supposed she would have to be polite about it. After seeing what Veronica could be like, she certainly didn't want her for an enemy. "I heard that," she said, trying to sound interested. "I've heard you were a good rider."

Veronica nodded, looking pleased. "I don't like to brag," she said smugly, "but I was pretty good back then. I still am, actually."

Callie bit back a sigh as Veronica started to go into detail about her own illustrious riding career. Why were so many people only interested in talking about themselves?

Still, she had to admit that she was a little relieved to have George safely removed to the front seat. She was going to have to do something about him before things went any further. Starting with getting out of that weekend study date . . .

NINE

Lisa peered over the half door of Belle's stall. "Hi," she greeted Stevie, who was inside. "Need any help?"

Stevie glanced up and smiled at her. "No thanks," she said. "I've got things under control in here." She hoisted a saddle onto Belle's back and started fiddling with the girth.

"Okay." Lisa leaned on the half door. "So, any news from Phil?" She had come straight to Pine Hollow that morning. For one thing, she'd wanted to look in on Prancer. Now that she knew the mare was going to be hers someday, it seemed even more important to monitor her pregnancy carefully. But first Lisa had made a point of tracking Stevie down to find out if there had been any new developments the night before. When she'd spoken to Alex on Sunday night, Stevie hadn't heard anything from Phil. And later that evening, Lisa's mother had closed herself off in her room and spent the rest of the night gabbing on the phone. Lisa hadn't wanted to interrupt her—especially if she was talking to Aunt Marianne, who always put her in a gloomy mood.

Stevie gave Belle's girth a yank and then glanced up at Lisa. "Tons of news," she announced, ignoring the bay mare, who was giving her a disgruntled look over her shoulder. "Mind if I keep working while I talk? Belle and I have to get cracking if we're going to be ready for that show next month."

"I don't mind," Lisa replied. "What are you going to work on today?"

"Review." Stevie took her lower lip in her teeth and, with some effort, tightened the girth another notch, moving easily with Belle as the mare took a step sideways. "I want to see what we need to work on most."

Lisa nodded. "So anyway . . ."

"Right," Stevie said briskly, reaching for Belle's bridle, which was slung over the door near Lisa. "Anyway, Phil finally called late last night—he and A.J. spent almost all night talking." She shrugged. "Once A.J. starts talking, he really starts talking."

"Wow. So did Phil get all the details?" Lisa hesitated, remembering how secretive A.J. had been lately. "And are we all allowed to hear about it?"

"Yep." Stevie slipped off Belle's halter as she

talked. "A.J. told Phil he doesn't care who he talks to about this, just as long as his parents don't find out." She shrugged. "He's still pretty steamed at them, though it doesn't sound like he's holding any grudges against us for dragging the truth out of him."

"So what is the truth?" Lisa asked. "How did he find out he's adopted if his parents didn't tell him?"

"Open your mouth, you big stubborn thing," Stevie ordered Belle, who was shaking her head, refusing to take the bit. Finally Stevie stuck her thumb into the corner of the mare's mouth, and Belle gave in with a snort. Once the bit was in place and the crown piece was fastened behind her ears, Stevie glanced at Lisa again. "Sorry about that," she said. "She's feeling kind of feisty today."

Lisa grinned. As far as she could tell, Belle felt feisty every day. That was one reason the horse was a perfect match for Stevie.

"Anyway," Stevie continued as she pulled Belle's forelock out from beneath the browband, "it's really kind of weird how he found out. His biology class was doing some kind of project on blood types, and he was supposed to find out his type and his whole family's. Well, I guess his dad didn't realize what that stuff can mean." She shrugged. "You know Mr. McDonnell is totally hopeless with anything scientific or medical."

"Which is why it's a good thing he's an English teacher," Lisa said absently. She had already figured out what came next. "So let me guess. A.J. found out he couldn't possibly be his parents' biological child because their blood types weren't compatible."

"Right." By that time Belle's bridle was on. Stevie gave her horse a pat, then turned to Lisa. "After he found out about that, he decided to poke around a bit on his own. I guess he still hoped there might be some mistake—maybe his dad had given him the wrong information or whatever." She shook her head, looking grim. "But I think he must have been pretty suspicious. He actually skipped school one day to go through his parents' files while they weren't home."

"Wow."

"Right. I think he probably just intended to go in late after he found out what he wanted to know." Stevie reached up to scratch Belle's forehead as the mare nudged at her with her big, soft nose. "But when he found the actual adoption records, it just blew him away. And the rest is history."

"Poor A.J." Lisa bit her lip, imagining what it must have been like for A.J. to make that discovery all on his own, without any support from family or friends. "He's spent all this time shutting everyone out, when he must have been going crazy wondering about all those things adopted kids supposedly worry about. Like why their biological parents gave them up, and where they really came from . . ."

"Uh-huh. Oh, I almost forgot," Stevie said. "While he was looking through the files, A.J. also found his little sister's birth certificate. She *is* their parents' biological kid. Which seems to have hit him pretty hard, too. Phil said A.J. was worried that his parents had stopped loving him as much when their 'real' child was born. His word, not Phil's, by the way."

Lisa nodded, trying to take it all in. "Why didn't his parents ever tell him about this?"

"Who knows?" Stevie scratched her ear absently. "Maybe they never found the right time. Maybe they figured they never needed to tell him—I mean, with that reddish hair of his, he definitely *looks* like his dad's biological son." She shrugged. "Whatever they were thinking, though, I guess it backfired. He's really angry that they never told him the truth. Makes it all seem that much worse, I guess."

Lisa noticed that Stevie was starting to get the fidgety look she often got when she was itching to get started on whatever task she had planned.

"You'd better get going," she said tactfully. "You don't want to keep Belle waiting, do you?"

Stevie sent her a grateful look. "I probably should get out of there," she agreed. "We can use all the practice we can get if we're going to do our part to uphold Pine Hollow's illustrious name. We'll talk more later, okay?"

Once Stevie and Belle had gone, Lisa wandered toward Prancer's stall nearby, still thinking about A.J. After hearing what Stevie had just told her, she could understand why A.J. had been so upset all this time. It must hurt to have to wonder where you came from, what your earliest days had been like, why the people who were supposed to love you more than anyone had decided to give you away instead. In A.J.'s case, the fact that his adoptive parents hadn't said anything to him about his origins must have been an additional kind of pain. Lisa thought she knew a little bit about what he was feeling—she had felt terribly hurt and betrayed when she'd realized that her parents' marriage wasn't as strong and permanent as they had always led her to believe it was.

Lisa had had to work through those feelings on her own, but it had helped a lot to know that her friends were there, supporting her, ready to help if they could. Now she wanted to make sure that A.J. knew they were there for him, too. Maybe she could even find a way to help him come to terms with his newly discovered identity. She decided to hit the public library that afternoon or the next and see what she could find out about adoption. A little research would help her understand A.J.'s feelings better.

When she reached Prancer's stall, the mare was dozing in the back corner. Lisa whistled softly to wake her, then slipped inside as the mare swung her head around to look at her. "Hey, Mama," she murmured, running her hands down the mare's neck and over her side. "How are you feeling?"

Prancer merely blinked in response. Then she stretched her neck to snuffle at Lisa's pockets, obviously hoping for a treat. Lisa chuckled.

"Sorry," she said. "I don't want to feed you anything unless I check with Max first." *Even if you are going to be mine someday,* she added silently, unwilling to expose the thought to the air even in the privacy of the stall.

Now that she'd had some time to adjust to Carole's news, Lisa was starting to think more about the practical aspects of owning Prancer. While part of her was thrilled that her father wanted to surprise her that way, another part couldn't help wondering if he'd really thought the plan through.

If I end up going to college anywhere in this area, Prancer could just stay here at Pine Hollow, she thought, still stroking the mare's face gently. *I could even arrange for Max to keep using her for lessons so she'd be sure to get enough exercise when I'm busy with midterms or whatever.*

Her thoughts continued along the familiar path she'd mapped out in the past couple of days. *Or I could end up at a school in California,* she thought. An image of Alex's unhappy face flashed into her mind, but she pushed it aside. She could only deal with one problem at a time. *That would work out okay as far as Prancer is concerned, too. Dad could help me arrange to board her somewhere in the area, and he and Evelyn could check on her when I come back East for holidays and stuff.*

She sighed as her thoughts moved on to the last part of the equation. *But not all the schools I'm interested in are around here or in California. What if I decide I want to go to college in Boston or Chicago? What would I do about Prancer then?*

As usual, no satisfactory answer presented itself. She sighed again and ran her fingers through Prancer's forelock.

"What do you think, girl?" she whispered. "What should I do?"

"Yo!" Alex's breathless voice came from outside the stall. "There you are. I've been looking all over for you!"

Lisa turned, caught between guilt for what she was thinking and joy—the joy she always felt when Alex was around. "Hi," she said, hurrying over to give him a kiss over the half door of the stall. "What are you doing here? I thought you and your buddies were studying for the PSATs this afternoon."

"Heh heh," Alex cackled diabolically. "That's exactly what I wanted you to think. That way I knew you'd be extra surprised when you saw *these*." With a flourish, he pulled a couple of brightly colored strips of paper from behind his back.

Lisa peered at them for a moment before realizing what they were. Then she gasped. "You got tickets to the Berryville Fall Festival?" she cried. "I can't believe it! I thought they were completely sold out!"

Alex shrugged. "Hey, I couldn't let that stop me," he said. "Not when my one and only was dying to go."

Lisa grabbed him and pulled him toward her so that she could kiss him again. Pressing her lips against his, she did her best to put every bit of her appreciation, anticipation, and love into the kiss. "Thanks," she murmured when they came up for air. "Did I ever tell you you're the best boyfriend in the whole world?"

"Not often enough." Alex grinned. "But if you kiss me again like that, I just might start to believe it."

"One, two, one, two, one, two," Stevie counted softly in time with Belle's steady trot. She smiled when she signaled for a transition and the mare responded instantly, moving effortlessly into a smooth canter. Once again, Stevie counted along. "One, two, three, one, two, three . . ."

Stevie had been working in the ring with her horse for nearly half an hour, and she was enjoying herself immensely. Judging by Belle's alertly pricked ears and the perfect cadence of her gaits, the horse was enjoying the workout, too.

Stevie realized it had been too long since she and her horse had spent an entire workout concentrating solely on dressage. *That's probably because I haven't entered a show since last spring,* Stevie thought, breaking off her counting and just feeling the rhythm of the pace for a moment. *That's way too long.*

She sighed happily, imagining how much fun it was going to be to compete at Colesford. Stevie knew that most people didn't understand why someone like her got such a kick out of dressage. It was such a disciplined, formal, *quiet* sort of event—hardly what one might expect from a fun-loving, sometimes downright boisterous girl like Stevie.

She didn't usually try to explain, preferring to leave people wondering. But the truth was, she loved dressage exactly because it was so quiet, so controlled. Becoming one with the horse, in total communication and concentration, was a challenge that paid off in a wordless partnership, a balance of control and self-control, grace and athleticism. Stevie had never known anything like it. When she and Belle were moving in complete harmony as they were at the moment, she felt a special joy and contentment.

She started asking Belle to lengthen and shorten her strides. Again the mare responded perfectly to each almost imperceptible aid. *Who knows?* Stevie thought optimistically. *Maybe we have a chance for a ribbon after all.*

As unlikely as that was, she enjoyed imagining it. After a moment, though, her mind turned to the other Pine Hollow entrants. Any one of them could easily take home a ribbon or two. Denise McCaskill was practically a shoo-in, especially paired with Talisman. Stevie had often wondered why Denise even bothered to remain at her job managing Pine Hollow when she could almost certainly make a living as a competitive rider.

Then there was George. Walking around on his own two legs, he didn't look like much. In fact, Stevie had often been struck by his resemblance to a sack of flour with a pumpkin balanced precariously on top.

I guess I must subconsciously be looking forward to Halloween already, she thought with a grin as she formed the image. *But it really does describe George's physique pretty well.*

Still, she had seen the sudden transformation he underwent whenever he climbed into his horse's saddle. Suddenly he seemed a little slimmer, a bit taller, his head a tad better proportioned. But the biggest change was in his carriage and attitude. He carried himself as if he belonged in the saddle, as if riding were much more natural to him than walking. That was why he did so well in dressage, as well as other disciplines. When he entered the ring on his beautiful Trakehner mare, there could be no doubt in any judge's mind that the two of them were in perfect harmony.

When it came to harmony between horse and rider, though, Stevie had never seen anyone quite like Ben. While George had a wonderful rapport with Joyride, Ben seemed to share a deep, special relationship with every horse he encountered. That quality would make him a formidable competitor in the Colesford show, just as it made him an excellent stable hand and trainer.

Too bad he can't get along with people anywhere near as well as he does with horses, Stevie thought as she signaled Belle for a walk. *The only people he seems to like at all are ones like Max and Carole who never talk about anything but horses.*

At that, her thoughts turned to Carole. Stevie had always known that her friend had a special passion and gift for working with horses. Now, perhaps, Carole would get her chance to show the world what her best friends had always known—just how special she was.

Stevie smiled as she remembered how excited Carole had been when Max had given them all the news. Maybe she hadn't whooped and hollered as much as Stevie herself had, but her deep brown eyes had taken on that soft glow they always got when she was really happy. In fact, her whole face had seemed to glow with joy and anticipation.

It's too bad she can't ride Starlight in the show, Stevie mused. *Luckily she seems to be taking it really well. I guess for her, riding Samson will be almost as special as riding Starlight would be.*

She thought back to the last time she'd seen Carole riding her own horse. To her surprise, she had to go back quite a way. She frowned, suddenly wondering about that. Once upon a time, hardly a day had passed when Stevie didn't see Carole in Starlight's saddle. But now . . .

I guess I haven't been coming to the stable every day, and when I come I haven't stayed that long, she told herself, leaning forward to give Belle a pat on the neck. *I've been pretty busy lately, and I suppose Carole has, too. For one thing, Max is keeping her tied up with Samson's training . . .*

Still, she couldn't quite dismiss that jarring feeling of surprise when she realized how little she'd actually seen of good old Starlight lately. It was really kind of odd when she thought about it.

Suddenly realizing that Belle was still walking steadily and patiently around the ring as her rider sat lost in thought, Stevie quickly focused her attention and asked for a trot. "One, two, one, two," she murmured.

A noise made her glance over at the fence. A small group of younger riders had just emerged from the stable building and were playfully elbowing and shoving each other as they wandered down the gravel driveway. As Stevie looked on, a skinny boy with brown hair tugged on a girl's long blond ponytail, then jumped away as she turned and came after him. Instead of smacking him, though, she grabbed him in a big hug while their friends all laughed.

"Ah, young love," Stevie murmured, amused. The kids were about Michael's age, she realized. At that thought, her slight smile widened into a full-fledged grin. She had been concentrating so hard on what she was doing that for a while she had almost forgotten about her little brother's new romance.

But now that she remembered, her mind was clicking into gear. The possibilities were endless. She couldn't wait to get home and start making his life completely miserable.

TEN

"Stevie," Mrs. Lake said wearily, pushing a strand of wavy blond hair out of her eyes, "didn't anyone ever tell you that Sunday is supposed to be a day of rest? So give it a rest, okay? Please."

Stevie just grinned and leaned back in her chair. "Sure, Mom," she said casually. "I'll give it a rest. Just stop *fawn*ing all over me, okay?"

"Mo-o-om!" Michael protested loudly, looking up from his afternoon snack of chocolate-chip ice cream washed down with ginger ale.

Mrs. Lake rolled her eyes. "Sorry, Michael," she said. "You're on your own. I've got to finish reading this case, and I don't think it's going to happen while I'm in the same room with Stevie." Quickly gathering up her papers from the kitchen table, she headed out of the room and toward the den.

After she'd gone, Stevie leaned over the table,

gazing at Michael. "So I'm finally alone with my *deer, deer, deer* little brother."

Michael shot Stevie a sour look. "You're so mature," he muttered.

"Yo," Chad said, hurrying into the room. "Any ice cream left?" Without waiting for an answer, he buried his head in the freezer and starting poking around among the contents.

"Don't you ever get anything to eat at college?" Stevie asked Chad, just as her twin entered with a soccer ball tucked under his arm.

"Did you find the ice cream?" Alex asked Chad. He glanced at Michael. "Hey. What's with you?"

"What do you mean?" Michael snapped.

Stevie winked broadly. "It's nothing. The *deer* little fellow's just pining away for his sweetheart." She hopped out of her seat and headed for the kitchen phone. "Maybe I ought to call her up and tell her how much he misses her."

"Stevie!" Michael howled, leaping out of his chair and racing across the room, just barely beating her to the phone. He grabbed the receiver and held it up threateningly. "You wouldn't dare!"

"Don't tempt me, deerie," Stevie remarked, swiping the ice cream carton out of Chad's hand on her way back to the table.

Alex loped over and grabbed it back. "Give him a break, Stevie," he said, tossing the ice cream to

140

Chad. "Don't you think you've been a little harsh these past couple of days?"

"Nope." Stevie folded her hands on the table in front of her. "I think I've been just harsh enough." She grinned, feeling very pleased with herself. For the past twenty-four hours, she'd made a point of dialing their own home number from the phone in her room, which luckily was on a separate line, and pretending it was Fawn calling for Michael. Once she'd pretended to ask him to elope with her. Another time she'd improvised a mushy love scene from *Bambi*. Most of the time she'd just started making kissing noises as soon as he picked up. The best part had been when Fawn herself had actually called the evening before and Michael had hung up on her. It was only when he'd turned around and seen Stevie grinning at him from a few feet away that he'd realized the truth and locked himself in the closet with the phone to call Fawn back.

Then there had been Stevie's brilliant idea to call up a local radio station during its weekly Romance Hour and dedicate a song from Michael to Fawn, "with hugs and smooches." *If I do say so myself,* she thought with satisfaction, *it was an extra touch of brilliance to request that gooey new love song, "Please Touch Me." He'll never live that one down!*

Stevie sighed with happiness as she thought

about it. Michael's face had turned such an interesting shade of purple when she'd pointed out that a lot of the girls in his class probably listened to that program. Maybe even Fawn herself . . . Stevie hadn't had this much fun in a long time. Why had she ever stopped playing tricks on her brothers? It was so . . . *satisfying*.

"Catch you later, guys," Chad said, shoveling one last bite of ice cream into his mouth and then shoving the carton toward Alex. "I've got to head downtown and meet my ride back up to school."

"See you," Alex said, and Michael grunted, which might have been meant to pass for some kind of farewell.

"Bye, Chad," Stevie added cheerfully. "Don't be a stranger up there at that college of yours. We're all awfully *fawned* of you, you know."

Chad just grimaced and loped toward the back door, stepping over Bear, who was snoozing in his favorite spot just in front of the door.

"Hmmm." As she watched her brother go, Stevie's gaze landed on the big golden retriever. "Hey, Alex," she said, casting a sidelong glance at Michael. "Did you ever notice that Bear's fur is kind of *fawn*-colored?"

Alex snorted. "Whatever," he said. "Listen, did Lisa mention her Emily party idea to you?"

"Sure. I think it's a cool idea." Stevie drummed her fingers on the table. "I thought we could have it here. But it's got to be soon—Emily's shipping out in, like, hours. At least that's how it feels."

"I know," Alex said. "I was thinking maybe we could do it a week from next Saturday. A little early for Halloween, but hey, I doubt anyone will complain."

Stevie nodded. "Sounds good. We ought to make it a really big bash—you know, send Emily off in style." She shrugged. "Besides, a big, fun party will probably be good for A.J., too, now that he's actually socializing again." She winked at Michael. "He's not the only one, eh, lover boy?"

Alex rolled his eyes. "Yeah," he said shortly. "Well, we can talk about the party plans later, okay? I've got to go get ready for that PSAT course this afternoon." He took off.

Stevie shrugged. What was his problem? She was going to the two-hour course too, but they didn't have to leave for almost an hour. And the only thing she planned to do to prepare for it was put on her shoes.

He's probably going to spend the next forty-five minutes combing his hair just perfectly, in case he runs into Lisa on his way out, she thought with a snort. *I guess that's the drawback of living a few doors down from your girlfriend.*

That brought her mind back to another neighborhood romance. She hopped out of her chair and headed for the stairs. It was time to call Michael again.

As she locked her car and walked across the tiny, weed-infested parking lot that the Willow Creek Public Library shared with several other downtown buildings, Lisa was thinking hard about adoption. She realized it was a topic she'd never really considered much before. What would it be like, not knowing who had given birth to you? Knowing that somewhere, someone shared your genes—and you didn't even know them?

She couldn't imagine it. But she knew that lots of babies were adopted every day, so she guessed she wouldn't have any trouble finding information on the topic. She figured she'd start in the psychology section, then move on to periodicals.

And as long as she was at the library anyway, she figured she'd check out the college reference section one more time. She wanted to make sure the list of schools she'd come up with a few weeks earlier still seemed right to her now that she knew about Prancer.

Of course, Prancer's not the only one with an interest in where I end up next year, she thought with a little sigh. She and Alex had had a wonderful time at the concert in Berryville the evening before, but the secrets between them—the California secret, and now the college secret, which Lisa hadn't even realized she was keeping until the Prancer issue had come up—had gnawed at her even as she'd swayed along to the fantastic music. Would Alex understand if she decided to go to school in California? Would he understand if she went to Boston? No matter how great each band was or how addictive the beat, she hadn't been able to relax and enjoy herself completely at the fall festival, not with those kinds of questions hanging over her head.

It had almost made her sorry that she hadn't gone to the library the day before instead of going to the concert. Maybe she could have resolved at least the college part of the secret. Maybe she would have realized that those schools in Boston and California didn't offer the courses she wanted or the facilities she needed, and that she'd be better off at a school closer to Willow Creek. . . .

Not likely, Lisa told herself ruefully as she turned up the cracked back walkway. *But at least I would know what I faced right now and wouldn't still be wondering.* Besides that, today was one of Mrs. Atwood's rare weekend days off, and Lisa was sure her mother was disappointed that Lisa wasn't staying home to hang out with her. When Lisa had announced her plan that morning, the strange expression on her mother's face had almost convinced her to put her library visit off for another day. But she couldn't. College worries aside, A.J. was hurting now, and Lisa wanted to help him as soon as possible. If she found out anything helpful, she could call him that night and talk to him about it.

She stepped around an overgrown shrub and came in sight of the library's back door. "What?" she said aloud, stopping short and staring. A large white sign was taped to the inside of the glass. LIBRARY CLOSED FOR FUMIGATION, it read in big block letters. OPEN MONDAY.

Lisa was disappointed, but there wasn't much she could do. *I'll have to stop by the school library tomorrow before homeroom,* she told herself resignedly. *Or maybe wait until my study hall on Tuesday.*

She sighed as she turned and made her way back to her car. Fishing her keys out of her pocket, she unlocked the door and slid inside. After she'd started the engine, she sat there for a moment without putting the car into gear. Suddenly she had the whole afternoon stretching in front of her. What should she do now? Alex and Stevie were at a PSAT prep course, Carole was almost certainly at the stable. . . .

For a moment she toyed with the idea of swinging by Pine Hollow to see Carole—and Prancer. Then her mother's face, lonely and sad, popped into her head and she changed her mind. Imagining how surprised her mother would be to have her home today after all, she shifted into gear and drove out of the lot, turning the wheel for home. She could see Prancer anytime. Soon she would literally be able to see her anytime she wanted, ride her anytime she felt like it. . . .

Despite all the new problems her father's surprise gift had brought up, Lisa couldn't help smiling as she imagined owning the elegant bay mare. For one thing, it made it a lot easier to face months and months of riding other horses during Prancer's pregnancy. Before, Lisa hadn't been sure she could face that, since she would be off at college by the time the mare was ready to be ridden again. But now all she had to do was wait it out, knowing that they would have all the time in the world once Prancer's foals were weaned.

She was still thinking about that as she turned into her driveway. In fact, after thinking through her schedule for the coming week, she had decided to squeeze in at least one good trail ride as soon as she could, maybe Wednesday or Thursday. It would be nice to get out there in the woods again—she hadn't been spending nearly enough time on horseback lately, and she suddenly realized how much she missed it. Parking her car in the garage next to her mother's, she hurried toward the back door and let herself into the kitchen.

Almost immediately, the sound of muffled laughter met her ears. It was coming from the direction of the living room. For a moment Lisa assumed it was the radio or TV. But then her mother's voice rose clearly in another peal of merriment.

Perplexed, Lisa walked through the kitchen and into the hall. Had Aunt Marianne dropped by for a surprise visit, all the way from New Jersey?

The laughter faded away as Lisa reached the arched entrance to the living room. Her jaw dropped at what she saw inside.

Her mother was sitting on the sofa—passionately kissing a strange man!

ELEVEN

"**M**om!" Lisa cried out involuntarily, her shock overcoming her manners. "What are you doing?"

Mrs. Atwood immediately pulled back her hands, which had been caressing the man's curly dark hair, and leaped to her feet. "Lisa!" she exclaimed, sounding startled and flustered. Her hands flew to her own face and hair and clothing, checking that everything was in place and as it should be. "Darling," she said breathlessly. "We—that is, I—didn't expect you home for a couple of hours."

Lisa wasn't looking at her mother anymore. She had turned to stare in shock at the man who had also risen from the sofa at her entrance, looking embarrassed. Lisa couldn't help noticing that he was tall and broad-shouldered, with angular, striking cheekbones and soulful dark eyes. She also couldn't help noticing that he was clearly in his early twenties. "Who are you?" she demanded.

"Uh, hi," the man said, running a hand awkwardly through his hair. "Um, I'm Rafe. I work with your mom. You must be Lisa. Your mother talks about you all the time."

"Really," Lisa replied.

"Sweetie." Mrs. Atwood had regained some of her composure, though she still looked uncomfortable, glancing from her daughter to Rafe and back again. "I was planning to tell you soon. You see, Rafe just started at the store a couple of weeks ago—he's working there part-time to help pay his way through college."

"College?" Lisa couldn't keep the disbelief out of her voice. Her mother—her own conservative, forty-something mother—had been locking lips with a *college boy*? Did he know how old her mother was? Did she know how old he was? How old was he, anyway—twenty? Nineteen? "You're in *college*?"

"Lisa!" Mrs. Atwood exclaimed, sounding angry.

Rafe moved to her side and put a hand on her arm. "It's okay, Eleanor," he said. "It's cool. I don't blame her for being shocked." He turned to Lisa. "I'm not as young as you're probably thinking," he told her. "I'll be twenty-five in February. I took a couple of years off to knock around, do my own thing. You know—do some surfing, bum around Europe for a couple of months. The

150

school of life, you know?" He laughed. "But hey, the guys who do the hiring at good companies aren't too impressed with that kind of stuff. So I just went back—started my junior year at NVU this semester."

Lisa's head spun. NVU was one of the schools on her list, the school where Chad Lake went. None of this was making sense to her. "Oh," she said, mostly because she felt she had to say something. Both of them were staring at her.

Things were starting to fall into place. Her mother's unusually good mood, all those late nights at the store . . . She glanced at her mother.

"Lisa, do you want to help me in the kitchen for a minute?" her mother asked.

Once they were safely in the kitchen, Lisa turned to her mother.

"So, is Rafe your—your *boy*friend?" she asked, unable to stop herself from putting extra emphasis on the *boy* part of the word.

Mrs. Atwood laughed uncomfortably, not quite meeting Lisa's eye. "We haven't put any labels on it, sweetie," she said. "Let's just say—well—that Rafe and I have been getting to know each other better, and, well—"

"Okay." Lisa waved a hand quickly, not wanting to hear any more. She had a pretty good idea what was going on, and it made her feel a little queasy. "Whatever. Your life. Your business."

"Lisa," her mother said, her voice taking on a pleading tone. "Why don't the three of us sit down, have a cup of tea or something, and talk?"

"Sorry," Lisa said, not sorry at all. The last thing she wanted was to take part in some awkward little tea party with the two of them. "I've got some studying to do."

She picked up her pace, making her escape before her mother could try to stop her, and didn't slow down until she reached her room. Racing inside, she collapsed against the back of the door.

I can't believe this, she thought, still not completely convinced that the scene downstairs had really happened. *Mom's dating someone so young that—that I could be dating him. Except that I could never take someone seriously who actually used the phrase* school of life *without the slightest sense of irony. . . .* She shook her head slowly. *What in the world is she thinking?*

The next morning Carole scurried into homeroom just as the bell rang. Flinging herself into her seat near the back of the room, she sat there panting for a moment as the PA system crackled to life for morning announcements. She could hardly believe she'd made it on time—she'd been sound asleep only twenty-five minutes earlier.

Her father had left the house very early for a breakfast meeting with one of his clients, so she'd had to get herself out of bed. Monday mornings were always tough—Carole knew she wasn't the only student who felt that way—but today had been especially difficult. The day before at Pine Hollow, Samson had had some trouble with the tighter turns during his afternoon training session. Normally Carole would have put off working on the problem for another day to give the horse a rest. But with the Colesford show coming up so soon, they didn't have the luxury of time. She had rushed through her other chores and a quick dinner of a sandwich begged from Max's wife so that she could work with Samson again in the early evening.

The later session had gone much better, and Carole had felt very pleased with herself as she gave the big black horse an extra-long grooming to reward him. It wasn't until she was leaving his stall at seven that she remembered she'd promised Max she would mix all the grain for the next week before she left that day. She had considered just leaving, pretending she'd forgotten, but in the end her sense of responsibility had won out. She'd dragged herself wearily to the grain shed, finally finishing the task at around eight-thirty—after more than twelve straight hours at the stable.

She smothered a yawn as the principal droned

on and on about some upcoming sports events. Carole listened with half her attention, wondering why school announcements seemed to have so little meaning to her this year. Why should she care about football games or the field hockey team's new uniforms? What difference did it make to her if the cafeteria was changing its menu or the homecoming committee meeting was postponed? She wished she could skip her last two years of high school and move straight on to the next step, an equine studies program at a good college. Why should she waste her time learning about algebra and Spanish and all sorts of other things she'd never need to know?

The principal's next announcement broke into her thoughts. "Don't forget, juniors," he boomed in his deep voice, "the PSATs are coming up this Saturday. Those of you with last names beginning with the letters *A* through *M*, your test will be given in the gymnasium of Creekside Elementary School, right here in Willow Creek. The rest of you will be taking the test in the auditorium of Cross County Middle School over in . . ."

Carole didn't hear the rest of the principal's instructions. Her mind was racing, and suddenly she felt wide awake.

The PSATs, she thought frantically. *I completely forgot those were coming up so soon!* Now that she thought about it, she vaguely remembered Stevie and Alex and Phil mentioning the test a couple of times lately, but she hadn't paid much attention. There had been too many other important things to think about.

But Carole knew this test was important, too. The PSATs were the practice run for the SATs— the standardized test that all the colleges looked at when they decided whether to let you into their school. Carole would need a good score if she wanted to get into a school with a competitive equine studies department. Besides all that, she certainly didn't want a repeat of what had happened with that history test the week before . . .

Fighting back a rising wave of panic, she thought about the coming week. Today was Monday, and she had promised Max she would help him order feed that afternoon. For a second she considered asking Ben to take her place so that she could exercise Samson and Starlight and then hurry home to work on those practice sheets her homeroom teacher had handed out. But then she remembered what had happened on Friday. The day before had been Ben's day off, and for once he had actually stayed away, so Carole hadn't seen him since their last awkward conversation in the car. This wasn't exactly a good time to ask him for a favor.

Sighing, she thought forward to the rest of the week. Tuesday she was supposed to help Red

O'Malley, the head stable hand and assistant in-structor, teach an adult riding class. Wednesday she had volunteered to take on the beginning rid-ers herself for the first time—she didn't want to back out of that. Maybe if she just took Samson for a quick hack along the road near the stable to accustom him to strange sights, sounds, and scents, she could get home in time to start study-ing before dinner. Thursday one group of inter-mediate riders had their lesson. After she helped Red get the class started, she would only have to take care of Samson and Starlight, along with her regular chores, so she should be able to leave a little early then, too, instead of putting in extra time practicing for the Colesford show as she'd planned. . . .

She sighed again. Why did everything always seem to happen at once?

As she left school on Tuesday afternoon, Stevie was feeling a little restless. It had been a long day, starting with a pop quiz in her first-period Span-ish class and ending with a tedious, argumentative meeting of the Fenton Hall student council, fea-turing a seemingly endless debate on how to spend the proceeds of the last school fund-raiser. Stevie had hardly been able to hold her tongue as the student body president, a perky, intensely popular senior named Trina Sullivan, had insisted that the cheerleading squad definitely needed new pom-poms to go with the new uniforms it had gotten the month before.

But now Stevie was free at last. The rest of the sunny afternoon stretched before her, and while she knew she ought to go home and put in some more time studying for the PSATs, she couldn't quite work up a sense of urgency about it. A good education was of the utmost importance to both her parents, so they had made sure that Stevie's sometimes haphazard study habits didn't slop over into her PSAT preparations. She and Alex had both had to endure weekly study sessions, supervised by one or both parents, for the past month, as well as a weeklong preparatory course that summer. At the PSAT review on Sunday afternoon, Stevie had been pleasantly surprised to find that it had all paid off—she and Alex had both been in much better shape for the test than most of the other students who'd showed up.

I think that deserves a little reward, she thought smugly as she headed for the student parking lot. She had the car that day, since Alex was getting a ride home with one of his teammates after soccer practice. That made Stevie feel even more inclined to take advantage of the beautiful autumn day and do something fun.

On impulse, she decided to drive over to Cross County and see if Phil was home. She hadn't seen him since Saturday—she'd wanted to give him plenty of time to spend with A.J.—and she'd only spoken to him on the phone briefly a couple of times.

She cranked up the radio as she headed out of town toward the highway, singing loudly to cover the static from the ancient speakers. She was feeling good. Annoying, pom-pom–obsessed student council presidents aside, her life was really going well these days. The PSATs were going to be a breeze. She was entered in the Colesford Horse Show. A.J. was starting to work on his problems. She was even pretty sure she'd aced that pop quiz in Spanish.

"Yo soy muy inteligente," she said aloud with a grin. *"¡Muy lista!"*

When she reached Phil's street—more of a country lane, really, with no sidewalks or streetlights and very few other houses—she slowed down and coasted past his driveway, checking for his car. It was parked in its usual spot, and a second later she spotted Phil himself. He was in the side yard between the slightly ramshackle detached garage and the Marstens' tiny orchard, kicking a soccer ball around with A.J.

Stevie smiled and swerved, parking the car haphazardly in the grass along the side of the road. Hopping out of the driver's seat, she pocketed her keys and hurried toward the two boys, who were looking her way.

"Hey!" she called. "Surprise! Thought I'd drop by and see what you were up to."

Phil came forward to meet her with a quick kiss. "Hi, Stevie," he said. "It's good to see you."

"Yeah, yeah." Stevie grinned at him and turned toward A.J. "Hi," she said. "How are you?"

A.J. shrugged. He wasn't really frowning, but he wasn't exactly smiling, either. "Fine," he said, dribbling the soccer ball between his feet. "How are you?"

"I'm good." Stevie took a step toward him. "I've been thinking about you, A.J.," she said, making her voice as kind and understanding as she could. "I want you to know, if you need someone to talk to—you know, besides Phil or whatever—I'm here for you."

A.J. glanced at her. "Thanks," he said shortly. Then he glanced at his watch. "Listen, uh, I'd better get going. I've got a history paper due tomorrow."

"Wait," Phil protested. "I thought we were going to work on that together."

"Thanks for the offer," A.J. said, kicking the ball toward Phil, who caught it expertly under one foot, "but I can manage on my own."

Stevie watched him go, feeling slightly hurt despite her sunny mood. "Was it something I said?"

she asked plaintively as A.J. hopped on his bike and pedaled off down the driveway. "I thought we made a breakthrough the other day."

"I thought so too. But now I'm realizing it's not quite as simple as that." Phil put a comforting arm around her shoulders as they watched A.J. round a curve in the road and disappear from sight. Then Phil sighed and turned his worried green eyes toward Stevie. "He talked a lot about the whole adoption thing that first day, like I told you. But the more time passes, the less he wants to discuss it. I thought just having it out in the open would help him start to deal with it, you know? But it really doesn't seem to have changed things that much."

They started walking slowly toward the house, Phil keeping his arm around Stevie even as he dribbled the soccer ball between his feet. "At least he's doing his homework," Stevie joked weakly.

"I hope so." Phil shook his head. "When I stopped by his place after school today, he was just lying in his room listening to music. I practically had to drag him over here to get some fresh air." He shrugged. "And when I asked if he'd said anything to his folks yet, he practically freaked out, like he was afraid I was going to march downstairs right then and give away his secret."

"Wow. So isn't he ever planning on telling them that he knows?"

Phil shrugged again. "I guess not anytime soon," he said wearily. "I think he's still not that happy about the rest of us knowing. When I tried to suggest he might feel better if he got it all out in the open with his family, he said he was tired of talking about it. He said he appreciates our concern and all that, but he wants to deal with this in his own way."

Stevie's heart sank. Suddenly the day didn't seem quite as bright anymore. What had really changed because of their efforts? Yes, A.J. had revealed his secret. But it hadn't made things right. It hadn't solved his problems or even made him feel much better.

"It's so frustrating," she said, leaning closer into Phil's embrace. "How can we help him through this if he won't let us?"

TWELVE

Stevie was still feeling a bit gloomy about A.J. as she sat in homeroom the next morning. As Miss Fenton began her morning announcements, Stevie tried to cheer herself up by thinking of new ways to torture Michael about his relationship with Fawn. The night before, after returning from Phil's, she hadn't had the energy to do much. Today she wanted to come up with something creative.

Maybe she could arrange to run into Fawn after school that day. Fenton Hall was divided into three separate sections for the elementary, middle-, and high-school grades. But all three were housed in the same huge, crumbling old stone building, and the middle- and high-school students were dismissed at the same time in the afternoon.

I could offer her a few handy pointers for getting along with Michael, she thought. *Like making sure to ask about that Spider-Man underwear he used to love so much, or bringing him his favorite fresh-baked rhubarb-and-chili-pepper cookies . . .*

Shivering with anticipation, she tuned back into Miss Fenton's voice. The headmistress was droning on about that Saturday's PSATs and various other dull topics. But suddenly her voice changed.

"Students," Miss Fenton said over the PA system, her words coming much more slowly, her tone more hesitant and solemn. Stevie raised an eyebrow and sat up a little straighter in her seat, wondering what was coming next. "I have some unfortunate news to share with you now. It seems that one of our most accomplished students is leaving us."

Stevie glanced around the room, wondering who it was. Nobody else seemed to have any idea, either. For once, the entire homeroom was riveted on the boxy gray speaker above the classroom door. Even the teacher was staring at it, looking surprised.

Miss Fenton paused, then continued. "I'm sure you all know Katrina Sullivan, our student body president. I'm sorry to tell you that her family has decided to move. Er, immediately. Katrina will be helping to pack, and so will not be returning to school."

Stevie was sitting bolt upright by now. "Trina's

163

moving?" she cried. All around her, her classmates were expressing their shock as well.

"Therefore," Miss Fenton's voice went on, "the office of student body president will be open effective immediately. I have decided to hold a special election to choose a new president. Since national Election Day is coming up shortly, I thought that would be an appropriate date. Anyone interested in campaigning for the position should stop by the office before the end of the day today so we can begin the process."

"Wow." Betsy Cavanaugh, one of Stevie's classmates, leaned toward her from her seat across the aisle. "You're on the student council, aren't you? What was that all about?"

"I don't know," Stevie admitted. "Trina didn't say a word about any of this yesterday at our meeting."

Betsy chewed on her lower lip, her eyes glowing with curiosity. "Nobody just decides to move overnight like that," she declared. "There must be more to this story. Maybe Trina's pregnant or something!"

Stevie rolled her eyes. Betsy had always loved to gossip. Still, Stevie had to admit that she had made a good point for once. Trina's sudden withdrawal did seem more than a little odd.

I'm sure whatever it is, someone will sniff out the

story soon enough, Stevie thought idly. *We'll all know all the details before long.*

Her mind was already moving ahead toward the more important part of what Miss Fenton had said. With Trina out of the picture, there was a chance that they could elect someone more qualified to her post. Someone who might actually accomplish something useful as student body president, rather than wasting all sorts of time and money on cheerleading uniforms.

For a moment Stevie was tempted to run for the office herself. She had plenty of ideas, and most of the other kids knew her even though she wasn't a senior.

But then she had a better idea. *Scott!* she thought. *It's perfect. Wasn't I just thinking that he'd make a much better president than Trina? Well, this is his chance. He may be new, but practically everyone knows him already. And he's such a natural politician, he'll have no trouble winning them over, despite anything that stupid newspaper article said. This could totally be his chance to redeem himself and his family.*

She grinned, pleased with her plan. Now all she had to do was convince him to run.

A little later that day, Carole sat in her fourth-period study hall trying to cram as many vocabulary words into her head as possible. It wasn't easy—a few yards away, a couple of other students were giggling at each other endlessly, stopping only to kiss every time the teacher's back was turned. On the other side of the room, another student hummed tunelessly as he flipped pages in a car magazine. Besides all that, Carole's mind kept wandering—first to Pine Hollow or Samson or Colesford, then to the days and hours ticking away until she had to take the PSATs, then to the bleak future she would face if she bombed on the test, was totally unprepared for the SATs, and couldn't get into any colleges when she applied the following year.

Enervate. Enervate. Carole's mind went blank. What on earth did *enervate* mean? She had no idea. Flipping through the review book to the answer section, she quickly found the word. *To enervate,* she read. *To cause a reduction of mental, physical, or moral vigor.* She squeezed her eyes shut, willing her brain to soak up and retain the definition. Maybe thinking of it in a sentence would help her remember, she decided. *Enervate,* she thought. *Studying for the PSATs enervates me.*

She sighed, her gaze wandering to her algebra book, which was on the top of the stack of books poking out of her backpack. She knew she should probably put the PSAT book away and review those algebra problems she had to turn in sixth period. The afternoon before, after a group of riding students had finally finished their class and gone away, she had spent quite a bit of time in Max's office filling out the Colesford entry forms. Max had also wanted to talk to her about Samson's training schedule, and she hadn't been able to resist giving him a complete rundown of everything they'd done lately and everything she had planned for him between then and the show. Then after longeing Starlight for twenty minutes or so, she'd still had a few additional chores to do. By the time she'd arrived at home and gulped down the spaghetti her father had made, she had been so exhausted that she'd barely managed to scribble out a few answers to the math problems. She felt guilty about that, especially because of that history test, which seemed to pop into her mind every other second these days.

Still, it's just a few homework problems, she told herself, looking away from the algebra book. *It's not like blowing off studying for a test, or even a quiz. And the PSATs are important. I've got to do well, and I don't have much time.*

Mostly satisfied with that logic, she turned her attention back to the vocabulary list. But she still had trouble concentrating. Her schoolwork was really starting to feel out of her control, and she didn't like it. As much of a chore as it was, she was going to have to start buckling down and taking it more seriously. The best PSAT score in the world wasn't going to help her if she flunked out of eleventh grade. Not to mention the fact that Max would banish her from Pine Hollow if her average slipped below a C. Wasn't that why she'd done what she'd done two weeks before on that history test? She couldn't go through anything like that again. She had to keep her grades up from now on.

As soon as the PSATs are over, she told herself firmly, *and the Colesford show, I'm going to start putting more time into my schoolwork.* She nodded to herself, remembering one of her father's favorite phrases: *No ifs, ands, or buts about it!*

Stevie spotted Scott's familiar face among the crowds in the hallway between fourth and fifth periods. She hurried to catch up to him, not realizing until too late that he was walking with Veronica diAngelo.

"Oh," Stevie said, stopping short in front of the pair. "Uh, hi."

Veronica didn't bother to answer. She was hanging on Scott's arm, that repulsively flirtatious smile of hers aimed directly at him. To Stevie's disgust, Scott didn't seem to mind. He was smiling good-naturedly as usual.

"Hey, Stevie," he said cheerfully. "What's up? Ready for that lab report today in chem class?"

"Huh?" Stevie said distractedly. "Oh, uh, sure.

Whatever." She glanced at Veronica, wishing she would go away so that she could talk to Scott in private. But that wasn't likely, so Stevie plowed on. "But listen, Scott, I've been looking for you since homeroom. I wanted to talk to you about that open office for student council president. Um, I was thinking, you're already so popular, and everyone seems to like you and everything, and, well, I bet you're a whiz at making campaign-type speeches, and, well—"

Scott cut her off with a raised hand and a grin. "As much as I'm loving this flattery, you can save your breath, Stevie," he said. "You don't have to convince me. I've already decided to run."

"Really?"

Veronica smirked. "That's right," she told Stevie smugly, hugging Scott's arm a bit more tightly. "We were just discussing it. I think it's a wonderful idea."

Stevie ignored her. "But that's great!" she exclaimed, grinning at Scott. "You'll be a much better president than Trina was, and—"

"Speaking of Trina," Veronica interrupted, "did you hear what happened?"

Stevie realized in surprise that Veronica was talking to her. "What?" She'd almost forgotten the reason the office was open. She'd been too busy imagining all the wonderful things Scott could do as president—with her help and friendly advice, of course. But now she realized that she still didn't know why Trina's family was moving so suddenly. "Oh, uh, I guess not," she admitted. "Why? What happened?"

"I was just telling Scott about it," Veronica said with one of her superior little smirks. "I found out just a few minutes ago—hardly anyone knows the truth yet. I'm not even sure Miss Fenton knows the whole story."

Stevie gritted her teeth and did her best to be patient. "Yes?" she said.

"I don't know if you were aware of it, but Trina's father is a really high-ranking congressional aide." Veronica glanced up at Scott and winked, looking more self-satisfied than ever. "Or maybe I should say he *was* a congressional aide. It seems a reporter caught him last night taking part in some kind of major gambling ring. His boss didn't want to deal with the scandal, so he fired him right away, and the whole family's moving off to Kansas or Kentucky or somewhere in disgrace. I'm pretty sure it starts with a *K*. Anyway, they wouldn't let Trina come to school today because they didn't want the media to get hold of her."

As Veronica turned to greet a friend who was passing by, Stevie shot Scott a quick glance, surprised that with his family connections he wouldn't have heard about something like that before the rest of them. Catching her look, he winked and smiled slightly. Stevie realized he probably had heard about it first—and yet he was letting Veronica take all the credit for breaking the story. Stevie shook her head in amazement. As far as she was concerned, that was taking tact a little too far.

"Well, anyhow," she said, trying not to let her annoyance show. "The important thing is that she's gone. And like I said, you're going to make a much better president than she ever did."

"I haven't won the election yet," Scott said mildly.

Veronica poked him playfully in the shoulder. "Don't be silly," she said flirtatiously. "Who could possibly beat you? You're a sure thing!"

Scott shrugged. "I don't know about that. But I know one thing that might help my chances." He looked at Stevie seriously. "Would you be my campaign manager?"

"Your what?" Stevie could hardly believe her ears. True, she'd been planning to offer Scott a little strategic advice if he wanted it—after all, she'd attended Fenton Hall since kindergarten. She knew what the place was like. But taking on the job officially? Helping plan and execute the entire campaign? That sounded even better! "Definitely," she told Scott quickly, an eager smile spreading across her face. "I'd love to!"

"Great." Scott smiled back at her, looking pleased.

But not half as pleased as Stevie felt when she noticed Veronica's angry, envious scowl. *What do you know?* she thought happily. *The campaign hasn't even started yet, and I'm winning already!*

THIRTEEN

"Go!" Carole exclaimed a bit irritably. "You know Max will freak if you're late. So hurry!"

"Okay, okay." Juliet Phillips, a twelve-year-old intermediate rider, looked surprised at Carole's tone. But she scurried toward the outdoor ring with her horse, Pinky, in tow.

Carole blew out a long sigh, then pushed her hair off her face, feeling harried. The intermediate riding class was always a production—riders running late, unable to find their tack or their favorite hard hat or whatever. But today the students had seemed downright possessed. Rachel Hart had stumbled in the driveway and required soothing and some quick first aid; Sarah Anne Porter had practically gone into hysterics because she couldn't ride Barq that day; Juliet had been certain that Pinky had a fever, even though Carole could find no signs of illness whatsoever in the sturdy quarter horse. Even May Grover, usually one of the more sensible middle-schoolers around the place, had needed help untangling her knotted reins.

"Must be a full moon," Carole muttered as she turned her mind toward her next task—today's training session with Samson.

Thinking about the big black horse made her feel better immediately. That day she planned to work on circles and turns, and she was really looking forward to challenging his suppleness and obedience. Glancing outside to see which of the various rings and paddocks were free, she saw Scott Forester's sporty green car pulling into the driveway. Not wanting to spend valuable time chatting—she wanted to leave the stable at a reasonable time so that she could do some more studying for the PSATs that night—she hurried toward the tack room and grabbed Samson's saddle and bridle. Then she took the long way around to his stall, avoiding the aisle where PC was stabled. She couldn't help feeling a bit guilty about avoiding her friends that way, especially when she knew that Callie was kind of bummed out about Emily's imminent departure. But Scott could talk the spots off an Appaloosa, and she just didn't have time for it that day.

Her detour took her past Starlight's stall, and she paused to give her horse a quick pat. "Hey, boy," she greeted the bay gelding, who had his head out over the half door of his stall. "How's it going? Did you enjoy your day out in the fresh air?"

Starlight snorted and tossed his head, prancing a few steps sideways and almost running into the side wall. Carole frowned. Her horse seemed pretty frisky, despite the fact that she'd asked Denise to turn him out in the big meadow for the morning.

"Settle down, boy," she murmured anxiously as Starlight tossed his head again and pawed at the straw with one foreleg. He moved forward quickly and shoved insistently at her with his nose, leaving a trail of slobber down her arm.

She absently wiped the worst of it off on her shirt, still eyeing the big bay with concern. There was no doubt about it. Starlight was feeling particularly restless and mettlesome that day.

When was the last time I took him on a nice long ride? she wondered, thinking back. *I guess it's been quite a while. I've just been so busy. . . .*

But that was no excuse, and she knew it. One of the many responsibilities of horse ownership was making sure your horse got enough exercise, and Carole took that responsibility seriously. That was why she realized, with a sinking heart, that Starlight couldn't get by any longer with quick longeing sessions and leisurely days in a paddock or field. He needed to be ridden, and he needed to be ridden today. Otherwise he would soon be totally unmanageable. She bit her lip, already feeling one more precious hour slipping away. There was no way she could put in a full session with Samson now and still get in all the studying she'd planned. She couldn't possibly shirk on Samson's training with the Colesford show so close; but she also couldn't risk blowing the PSATs on Saturday.

Shaking her head, wishing she'd thought to volunteer Starlight to one of the intermediates for the day's class, she turned to race back to the tack room. She was thinking so hard that she almost ran smack into Lisa.

"Heads up!" Lisa exclaimed, jumping back just in time.

"Oh!" Carole had to scramble to avoid dropping Samson's tack all over the dusty aisle floor. She was startled by Lisa's sudden appearance, but she was almost as surprised simply to see Lisa at the stable. Carole hadn't noticed it consciously before, but her friend hadn't spent nearly as much time as usual at Pine Hollow lately. "Sorry about that. I guess I was—"

"In a hurry, as always," Lisa finished with a smile. "It's okay. I guess that means you're too busy for a trail ride today? I'm in the mood for a nice long ride."

"Sorry." Carole shook her head. "PSATs are Saturday."

That was all she needed to say. Lisa took that sort of thing more seriously than anyone, and she would be the last person to discourage anyone else from studying. "No, *I'm* sorry," Lisa said. "How could I forget about that? Alex has been studying like crazy for weeks." She shrugged. "I'll just go out by myself, okay? Consider this my notification. I'll probably take the mountain trail."

Carole nodded. The younger riders at Pine Hollow weren't allowed to ride alone on the miles of trails surrounding the stable, but high-schoolers and adults could go solo if they wanted to, as long as they notified a Pine Hollow staff member of their departure and planned route. That way, if they didn't return, Max would know where to send a rescue party.

Lisa took a few steps past Carole to pat Starlight, who had his neck craned toward them over the stall door. "Hey, fella," she greeted the gelding affectionately. Then she returned her attention to Carole, still automatically stroking the horse's neck as he snuffled at her pockets for treats. "So now that Prancer's confined to the maternity ward for months and months, I guess it's time for me to start getting reacquainted with some of the other horses. Who's available today?"

Carole shifted Samson's saddle to her other arm. It was nice to be able to discuss Prancer's condition openly. Max had finally announced the mare's pregnancy in last Saturday's Pony Club meeting, so the secret was out. "Let me think," she said, running a mental list of Pine Hollow's residents through her mind. "An intermediate class just started, so a lot of the usual suspects are tied up there—Eve, Diablo, Comanche, Checkers . . ."

Lisa was already nodding. "I saw them in the ring outside," she said. "What about Barq? He wasn't out there."

"He threw a shoe this morning. The farrier's coming by later. And Max doesn't want anyone riding Firefly until he gets Judy here to look at that nick on her leg."

"What about Windsor or Congo?"

"Not here. Mrs. Twitchett and some niece of hers took them out a few minutes ago." Carole frowned slightly as she realized what this all meant. There wasn't one appropriate school horse in the stable at the moment for Lisa to ride. Aside from Prancer, Samson, Barq, and Firefly, just about the only horses in their stalls were the resident stallion, Geronimo, and a handful of ponies. Plus the privately owned horses, of course, including Starlight.

"Oh." Lisa looked disappointed. "Well, I guess I should have called ahead. Too b—"

"Wait!" Carole had just had a flash of inspiration. "I know. Why don't you ride Starlight?"

"Starlight?" Lisa looked surprised and a little confused as she glanced over her shoulder at the tall bay, who was still stretching his neck out, enjoying her pats. "Me ride Starlight?"

"Why not?" Carole grinned, certain that she had hit on the perfect plan for all concerned. "He could use a good workout, but I'm really crunched for time today, so you'd be doing us both a favor. Plus you won't even have to pay for the ride, since he's my horse, not Max's."

Lisa looked thoughtful. "Are you sure?" she asked. "I mean, I wouldn't want you to miss out on—"

"Don't worry about it for a second," Carole interrupted. "Like I said, I'm crazed today. I have a million other things to do around here. And if I want to get home in time to study for my PSATs . . ."

"Okay, okay." Lisa finally looked convinced. "Thanks a lot, Carole. I really appreciate this." She turned to Starlight again. "How about it, boy? Feel like a nice long trail ride?"

Starlight snorted and tossed his head as if in reply, and Carole smiled. "I think that was a yes," she joked, feeling as if a weight had been lifted off her shoulders. With Starlight taken care of, she could turn her attention back to Samson, where it belonged. "See you two later, okay?"

An hour and a half later, Lisa gave Starlight one last pat. "Thanks for the ride, boy," she told the horse fondly. "Hope you had as much fun as I did." She picked up the gelding's grooming bucket and stepped out of the stall, latching it firmly behind her. Then she hoisted Starlight's tack from the wall where she'd left it and headed in the direction of the tack room. Dodging around a couple of stray riders hurrying toward the exit, she made her way across the entry area into the little hallway leading to the small, leather-scented room.

She set the saddle on a cleaning rack and hung the bridle on a free hook. Stretching to loosen her arm and shoulder muscles after the long ride, she grabbed a clean cloth from the pile near the sink and dampened it. Setting to work on the familiar task of wiping down the bridle, she allowed her mind to wander. She was still a little surprised at Carole's sudden generosity. Lisa had ridden Starlight on occasion in the past for one reason or another, but she'd rarely spent a leisurely afternoon on the trail with him. He was a wonderful, responsive horse and a pleasure to ride. She'd had such a good time with him that for a little while she'd even forgotten to worry about Prancer.

But now that she was back, her worries had returned full force. How could her father's wonderful, generous surprise gift be causing her so much consternation when she wasn't even supposed to know about it yet? Lisa wasn't sure. All she knew was that owning Prancer was going to make her life richer and more satisfying—and more difficult. After researching her college choices again that week, she'd come to the unsettling conclusion that a number of the schools she was most interested in were in places where keeping a horse nearby would be difficult and expensive, if not downright impossible.

How can I drag Prancer away from Pine Hollow and stick her in some dreary stable in the middle of Chicago or Boston? she wondered, glancing out the tack room's small windows at the idyllic rolling pastures and autumn-tinged trees beyond. *How can I trust her with strangers while I'm busy figuring out how to handle college myself? How can I—*

"Hi, Lisa." Callie's voice interrupted her thoughts.

Lisa looked up, startled. Realizing that her cleaning cloth, dry by now, was hanging idly in her hand, she smiled sheepishly. "Oops. Hi," she said. "Um, you caught me in the middle of a thought."

"So I see." Callie smiled back, moving carefully over the threshold on her crutches.

As she returned to the sink to wet her cloth again, Lisa thought about how much better Callie looked now than she had when Lisa had returned from California in August. She moved much more easily on her crutches and could support much more of her weight on her bad leg. Lisa was sure that Emily's careful attention during their months of therapeutic riding was at least part of the reason.

"Did you just finish a session with Emily?" Lisa asked as she returned to Starlight's bridle.

"One of the last." Callie's voice sounded sad as she began to clear PC's saddle, which was sitting on the rack beside Lisa's. "I still can't believe Emily's moving so soon. I mean, her good-bye party's in a little over a week!"

Lisa gave the other girl a sympathetic glance. They would all miss Emily, but Callie had more reason than most to be sorry she was leaving so soon. Why did so many of life's big changes always seem to happen at the worst possible times? "I guess you can never be prepared for things like that," she mused, thinking more of her own questions about Prancer than of Callie. "It's hard to make plans when other people's plans are always changing."

"Tell me about it," Callie replied ruefully as she slowly rubbed a rag over PC's bridle. "I'd miss Emily anytime she moved, of course—she's a great person and a terrific friend. But if only her parents could have waited a few more months . . ."

If only my dad could have decided to buy Prancer for me last year, before Max bred her . . . , Lisa added silently. She knew that the few months' difference, that slight shift in timing, might not have solved all her difficulties. She would still have to reconcile owning Prancer with her college plans. But it would have been so much easier if she'd been able to keep that issue in mind all along, instead of having it thrown at her now, when she'd already narrowed down her list of schools, when she was already distracted by the serious health issues of the mare's carrying twins.

"I understand how you feel," Lisa told Callie, meaning it. "It's like you try to be so organized and everything, and then someone comes along and throws a wrench into the works. It doesn't seem fair sometimes."

"I know." Callie remained silent for a moment.

Lisa finished cleaning Starlight's bridle and moved on to the saddle, removing the stirrups and the girth. She was surprised that she and Callie were having such a serious talk. The two of them had felt a little awkward around each other ever since Lisa's return—Callie had gotten to know Stevie and Carole over the summer while Lisa was away, and so they'd been put in the uncomfortable position of having the same friends while knowing very little about each other.

But time and familiarity had eased the tension

bit by bit, and Lisa was surprised to find that she already had difficulty remembering why she'd ever resented Callie in the first place. It seemed almost natural to talk with her one-on-one this way, without their friends around to mediate.

"I guess life's never predictable, is it?" Callie said at last, interrupting Lisa's thoughts once again. "Just when you think you have it figured out—*bam,* it smacks you upside the head again."

Lisa guessed the other girl was thinking about the car accident that had caused her injuries as well as about Emily's departure. "Right," she agreed. "I never could have guessed some of the things that have happened lately, that's for sure."

"You mean Prancer's pregnancy?" Callie turned a shrewd eye toward Lisa.

Lisa nodded. "Definitely," she agreed, wishing once again she could share the other part of the Prancer secret. "It really took me by surprise."

"We were all pretty surprised by that one." Callie rubbed a sponge with saddle soap. "Especially about the twins thing." She chuckled and glanced at Lisa out of the corner of her eye. "I guess that was just Nature's way of adding another little twist to the surprise. Just to keep us on our toes, keep us from getting too comfortable and satisfied with things the way they are." She shrugged, her expression growing more serious once again. "Sort of like with me and Emily. I can't forget about my

184

goals just because she's leaving, just like you haven't given up riding because Prancer's out of commission for a while. We have to keep going, find a new way to deal with it all and move on."

Lisa nodded thoughtfully. She hadn't thought about it that way before. For some reason, it made her feel a bit better. Events might seem random, life might seem hard sometimes, but when it came right down to it, they were all in it together. Life didn't stop when something unexpected happened, which was scary but strangely comforting as well. Whatever happened, however impossible it seemed that things could ever work out, time marched on, carrying everyone along with it.

I've just got to keep that in mind for the next few months, Lisa told herself. *Time goes on. A year from now I'll probably wonder what on earth I was so worked up about. By then I'll be in college. Prancer will have had her foals. Alex and I will have figured out a way to be together. If I can just keep believing all that, I should be all right, no matter what happens in between.*

She knew that Callie wasn't going to let Emily's departure stop her from learning to walk without crutches. It sounded as though she was already coming to terms with it. Lisa admired her for that and vowed to follow her example if she could.

It may seem impossible right now, she told herself. *But things will work out for Prancer and me somehow. They've got to.*

Callie balanced her weight on her crutches as she hoisted PC's clean and shiny saddle off the cleaning rack. "All done," she told Lisa, who was picking at a stubborn piece of dirt on the cantle of Starlight's saddle. "Almost ready?"

"Almost." Lisa glanced up at Callie and took a step forward. "Need some help with that?"

"I've got it," Callie said quickly. Realizing her words might have sounded a bit brusque, she smiled at Lisa apologetically. "Thanks," she added, lifting the saddle to its rack on the tack room wall. "But I really can do it myself. It's good exercise."

Lisa nodded. "I understand. It's okay," she said. "Just give me a second and I'll walk out with you."

"Great." Callie turned away to hang her bridle on the appropriate peg beside the saddle. When she turned around again, she saw that Ben Marlow had appeared in the tack room door. "Hi, Ben."

Lisa glanced over her shoulder. Callie could tell she hadn't heard Ben come in. That was nothing unusual—Ben walked around the place like some kind of gloomy ghost, sometimes seeming surprised that the mortals around the place could sense his presence at all.

"Hey," he greeted the two girls in his usual dispassionate tone. "Max isn't in here."

It was a statement rather than a question, but Lisa shook her head. "Haven't seen him lately," she told Ben politely. "Have you checked up at the house? He probably needed a rest after both a beginner and an intermediate lesson today."

Ben inclined his head briefly in what could have been a nod. Suddenly he took a step toward Lisa, his gaze now trained on the tack in front of her. "Starlight?"

Lisa nodded. "I took him out on the trail today," she explained. "Carole was running late, and he needed exercise, and all the decent horses were tied up, so it worked out great for all of us."

Ben looked startled. "Was that your idea?" he demanded. "Or Carole's?"

Callie blinked in surprise at Ben's tone. He kept to himself so much that it was always a shock when he actually expressed an interest in what other people were doing. Still, she supposed that anything having to do with horses held at least some interest for him.

Lisa looked startled at the blunt question, too, but she answered cordially. "It was Carole's, of course," she said. "Like I said—"

"Right," Ben interrupted. He stared at the saddle again as if looking for answers in its softly gleaming brown leather.

"So?" Lisa was starting to look slightly annoyed by now, and Callie couldn't blame her. Ben's unique personality seemed to work for the horses he trained—they all adored him—but his odd, cryptic way of expressing himself hadn't won him many human friends as far as she could tell.

Ben shrugged, still staring at the saddle. "Strange," he muttered, looking more ill at ease with every word.

"It's not strange at all." Lisa was frowning by now, her hands on her hips. "Carole's got a lot going on this week—the PSATs, her job here, that horse show. And it's not like she's shoving her duties taking care of her horse off on some stranger, you know. I'm her best friend—I've known Starlight since the day she got him. She knows I love him almost as much as she does and that I'll take good care of him."

Ben scowled, shrugged, and backed out of the room without another word. Lisa glanced at Callie, shaking her head grimly.

"Can you believe him?" she said. "What business is it of his if Carole lets me ride Starlight? The way he was acting you'd think she was letting any old stranger take him out on the trail." She snorted. "He should know as well as anyone that

Carole treats that horse as if he were made of gold."

Callie just nodded and kept silent. Privately, she suspected that Lisa might have missed Ben's point. She seriously doubted that Ben was accusing Carole of neglecting her horse. As Lisa had said, he knew better than that—Carole took good care of every horse at Pine Hollow.

But maybe there was more to it than that. Wasn't it a bit strange that Carole had urged Lisa to ride Starlight that day? After all, from her position aboard PC in the main schooling ring, Callie had been able to see the paddock where Carole had been working with Samson, riding him in a seemingly endless series of turns and circles. In fact, she'd still been at it when Callie and Emily had quit for the day and come inside. Spending more than an hour riding one of Max's horses hardly seemed like the action of a girl who was pressed for time.

Still, she kept silent. Lisa had known Carole for years and years. If she didn't see any problem, who was Callie—or Ben, for that matter—to argue? It wasn't as though Callie herself had thought twice about the subject until Ben had brought it up. Besides, Carole was supposed to ride Samson in that big horse show just a few weeks from now. Callie knew how important it was to eke out every possible moment of training with your mount before an important event. She couldn't blame Carole for wanting to concentrate on Samson for a little while, even if it meant sacrificing a few pleasure rides on her own horse.

FOURTEEN
14

Stevie leaned back comfortably in her chair, propping one knee on the edge of the kitchen table and absently scratching Bear's head, which was resting heavily on her other knee. "So, Michael," she said casually, "I wrote a poem for you today during my study hall. Want to hear it? It's called 'I Wandered Lonely as a Fawn.' "

Michael shot her a dark look as he carried a dirty pan from the stove to the sink. "I wrote a poem, too," he grumbled. "Just now. It's called 'Stevie Is a Jerk.' "

Stevie grinned, knowing he was trapped for a little while at least. The family had just finished dinner, and it was Michael's turn to clear the table and load the dishwasher. Alex had gone outside to kick the soccer ball around in the last few minutes of daylight, and their parents had disappeared into the study to discuss some case or other.

That meant Michael was Stevie's—all Stevie's. "So maybe you're not in the mood for poetry right now," she said. "That's okay. We can change the subject if you want. Let's see, what could we talk about . . . Oh, I know. You heard we're having this party for Emily next weekend, right?" She and Alex had cleared the good-bye party with their parents earlier that evening, and she was looking forward to giving her friends the good news.

"Sure," Michael replied cautiously, glancing around from his position at the sink.

Stevie shrugged. "Well, we would invite you," she said, "but I'm afraid it's a no-smooching zone. So unless you and Fawn can promise to control yourselves . . ."

Before Michael could do more than scowl and roll his eyes, the phone rang. Stevie shoved Bear's head aside and leaned over to grab the receiver off the wall near the doorway. "Hello?" she said cheerfully, crossing her fingers and hoping it was Fawn.

"Stevie? Is that you?"

"Phil?" she said with a little frown, barely recognizing his voice. She hadn't spoken to him since she'd seen him on Tuesday afternoon. "What's wrong?"

"I need to see you." His words sounded so strangled with worry that Stevie's heart immediately started beating faster with concern. "Can you meet me somewhere? Right away?"

"Sure," Stevie replied, her hand gripping the receiver tightly. "But what is it? What happened?"

"I don't— Just meet me at that spot at the picnic grounds as soon as you can, okay?"

"Okay." Stevie knew exactly which spot he meant. There was a public picnic area along the highway in the state woodlands that separated Willow Creek from Cross County. Since the picnic area was halfway between their homes, Stevie and Phil often met there when they just wanted to hang out together. They'd adopted one particular table beneath a huge, spreading oak tree as "their" spot, spending many a long afternoon wrapped in each other's arms, perched on the rough wooden table in the dappled shade of the big tree. "I'll be there."

"What's the matter?" Michael asked sourly as she hung up the phone. "Does Phil want you to come meet him so he can break up with you? I don't blame him."

Stevie didn't bother to respond. Racing for the back door, she grabbed her jacket and car keys. Outside, she paused just long enough to tell Alex where she was going. Then she hopped into the car and took off for the highway.

She arrived at the picnic area ten minutes later and was out of the car almost before the engine sputtered to a stop. Phil was already standing in front of their table, looking very pale in the twilight, and she hurried to meet him.

"What is it?" she asked, taking in his tortured expression. "What's wrong?"

"It's A.J.," Phil said without preamble, his hands shoved deep into his pockets. "I—I think I just made a big mistake."

"What do you mean?"

Phil shrugged. "I ran into his parents at the grocery store," he said quietly. "They still had no idea what was wrong with him, and they just looked so hurt and sad. So . . . So defeated, or something. Like they'd totally given up on ever being happy again."

Stevie gently took his hand and led him to the picnic table. Perching beside him on the bench, she gazed at him seriously. "Did you tell them?" she asked, already knowing the answer from the look on Phil's face.

He nodded. "It seemed like the thing to do at the time." He swallowed hard. "I mean, I just couldn't lie when they asked me if I'd talked to him lately. Besides, they need to know, don't they? How else is A.J. going to get past this?"

"I think you did the right thing," Stevie said sincerely, rubbing the back of his hand gently. "He had to talk to them about this sooner or later. Why make everyone suffer longer than they have to? It was for his own good as well as theirs."

"Too bad he doesn't see it that way," Phil said glumly. "I guess they talked to him as soon as they got home. He called me up and practically screamed at me. Said I should have minded my own business and he wished he'd never met me. That kind of thing."

"Wow." Stevie shook her head grimly. "Still, you did what you had to do, right? I'm proud of you."

"You are?"

"Sure." She put her arm around his hunched shoulders. "It was totally brave and noble. You risked messing up your friendship, but you did it to save your friend. You *had* to do it."

"Thanks . . . I guess," Phil said, still looking worried. "I wish that made me feel better." He sighed wearily and rubbed his eyes. "Anyway, thanks for coming to meet me. For listening."

"Anytime," Stevie said, leaning over to give him a quick kiss on the forehead.

Phil brushed her hair out of her face and kissed her back on the lips. "Thanks," he said again. "Did anyone ever tell you you're the coolest?"

"Sure," Stevie joked breezily. "My other boyfriends tell me that all the time."

Phil chuckled. "They're right, you know." He kissed her again, then sat back a bit. "Anyway, so what's new with you?"

Stevie sensed that he didn't want to talk about

A.J. any longer. There was really nothing more to say that they hadn't said a hundred times before. He just needed confirmation from Stevie that what he'd done was okay. "Alex and I talked to Mom and Dad about the party today before dinner."

"What'd they say?"

"They said we could have it at our house," Stevie replied. "Was there ever any doubt?"

"Not really," Phil admitted with a hint of a smile. "When you set your mind to something . . . well, let's just say you can be very persuasive."

"Hey, is that a PSAT vocabulary word?" Stevie accused him.

Phil shrugged. "What can I say? After all that studying, I am the king of the English language."

Stevie grinned. "Oh, really?" she said. "Well, speaking of kings—actually, make that *presidents*—and persuasion, guess what happened at school yesterday?" She quickly filled him in on Trina Sullivan's sudden departure and Scott's decision to run for her vacated office. "So get this: Scott asked me to be his campaign manager!" She grinned. "Isn't that incredible?"

Phil looked taken aback. "What did you tell him?"

"I said yes, of course. It will be a blast!" Suddenly noticing that his expression hadn't changed, she added, "What?"

Phil shrugged. "Nothing," he said. "I'm just kind of surprised you'd want to take something like this on right now, that's all. You're pretty busy already these days, you know? School, the PSATs, the big horse show, Emily's party . . ."

Stevie hadn't really looked at it that way before. She did have a lot on her plate in the next few weeks. But she wasn't really worried. She never felt more energized and happy than when she was throwing herself wholeheartedly into fun, challenging, interesting things. The Colesford Horse Show, Scott's campaign, Emily's party all promised to be full of excitement, and she was looking forward to playing her part in every one. "Don't fret," she teased. "I'll always have time for you, you know."

She leaned over to kiss him again. She wrapped her arms around his neck, not planning to let him go for a good long time.

It was completely dark by the time Stevie approached the turnoff for Pine Hollow on her way home. On an impulse, she decided to stop in and say hello to Belle. She hadn't been to the stable in a couple of days, and she missed her horse.

The stable was hushed and dim when she entered, the aisles lit only by the safety lights, which stayed on all the time. Not bothering to flick on the brighter overheads, Stevie hurried across the entryway toward the stable aisle. When she turned the corner, she almost jumped out of her skin. Someone else was standing in the middle of the aisle.

"Hello?" she called uncertainly, startled to find anyone in the place this late, with no lights.

When the figure turned, she immediately recognized George Wheeler's pale, round face. He looked as surprised to see her as she was to see him. "Stevie?" he called back. "Um, hi. I didn't— that is, I wasn't—I didn't know anyone else was here."

"Neither did I." Stevie wondered what he was doing on this side of the stable. His horse, Joyride, was housed on the opposite arm of the U-shaped row of stalls. Reaching his side, she glanced curiously at the stall closest to him and met PC's placid face staring sleepily back at her. "I just stopped by to say hi to Belle."

George glanced at PC, looking embarrassed. "I—um, I came to check on Joyride. The farrier was here earlier, and I asked him to put new shoes on her if he had time."

"Oh." Stevie didn't bother to mention that they weren't anywhere near Joyride's stall. The fact was obvious. "Well, I guess I'd better be—"

"Stevie?" George interrupted suddenly, his

dimpled cheeks blushing a mottled pink. "Um, could I—I mean, I wonder if I could talk to you about something. It's—well, it's sort of private, but I thought you—that is, I just wanted to say it."

"Say what?" Stevie asked, feeling confused and uncomfortable. She'd never spent much time chatting with George, but as far as she knew he wasn't usually this incomprehensible.

George took a deep breath and glanced around. "It's kind of hard to talk about," he said in a stronger voice, seeming to take some strength from the cozy intimacy of the evening stable. "I've never really felt anything like this, and I—I'm not quite sure how to act. Or what to do. Or even if I should do anything at all. I mean, I know I'm not exactly the best-looking guy in the world, or—"

Suddenly Stevie realized what this had to be about. "Are you talking about Callie?"

George gulped. "How did you—I mean, I—"

"It's okay." Stevie smiled at him reassuringly. "I sort of suspected you liked her."

George's face turned a deeper shade of pink. "You did?" he said faintly. "How? I mean, I hope I haven't been—"

"Don't worry. You haven't been that obvious," Stevie broke in. "I'm sure Callie herself doesn't suspect a thing—I haven't breathed a word." She grinned at him. "But you're lucky I'd already guessed. The way you were talking, I might never have figured it out."

"I'm not very good at these things." George sighed, looking so sad that Stevie started worrying that she'd said something wrong.

"I'm sorry," she said quickly. "I wasn't making fun of you or anything. I know it's hard to talk about these things sometimes." *Especially to someone you barely even know,* she thought.

George seemed to have an inkling of her thoughts. "I know you and I don't know each other that well," he said, sounding a bit sheepish. "But I know you're friends with Callie. And at school you always seem . . . well, pretty confident and everything. I thought maybe you could help me. You know, give me some advice on what to do."

"Uh, sure," Stevie said dubiously. "But what—"

"It's my father's fault, really," George interrupted in a sudden rush. As soon as the words were out of his mouth his eyes widened, giving him the effect of a rabbit who'd wandered into a stampede. "Sorry," he said, gulping nervously. "I didn't mean to say that."

"Say what?" Stevie was feeling more and more confused. She wasn't really sure what George wanted from her. The only thing that was clear was that he was terribly stricken about something.

George chewed on a fingernail for a moment, seeming uncertain how to answer. He glanced around the quiet stable aisle once more. "My father—he and my mom are divorced now. I haven't seen him in a long time."

Stevie nodded, waiting for him to go on. She had no idea why he was telling her this, but she couldn't help being curious.

"He always likes to call himself a 'real man.'" A touch of bitterness came into George's voice. "He's really macho—the type of guy who never backs down from a fight, who never lets women or anyone else give him any bull." His mouth twisted in an ironic smile. "My mom didn't think much of that, I guess."

"Hmmm." Stevie wasn't sure what else to say.

George shrugged, his face pained. "I guess I was a big disappointment to him," he said softly. "I was never much into sports other than riding, which he considered a 'girly' thing to do. And I guess I—I used to cry too easily when I was little. When kids picked on me in school or whatever. He really hated that—used to say I was a big softy and I should've been born a girl."

"Wow." Stevie shook her head sympathetically. "Sounds pretty harsh."

George laughed self-consciously. "Sorry to dump all this on you," he said. "I just wanted you to understand why I—I never know what to say.

Around Callie, I mean. I—she's the first girl I've really—"

He broke off again, but Stevie nodded. "I understand," she said, though she wasn't quite sure she did.

"Please don't tell anyone," George said urgently. "What I've told you. About my father and—and Callie."

"I won't," Stevie promised. "You can trust me." She was feeling a bit uncomfortable with this whole conversation. Why had George decided to confide in her about something so personal? Why had he chosen to speak to her about his crush on Callie at all?

It would have been easier if she'd had the slightest suspicion that Callie might return George's feelings. If this had been Ben Marlow confiding an interest in Carole, for instance . . . Stevie shook her head slightly, trying to stay focused. What was her responsibility here? Most of the time she considered people's love lives their own business, to handle as they saw fit. But George was so earnest, so sincere and innocent and trusting. Should she really keep silent in this case, thereby tacitly encouraging him to continue a crush that was unlikely ever to be mutual?

What else can I do? she thought helplessly. *It's not my place to speak for Callie. I don't even know for sure that she doesn't like George.*

Moving past that last thought, which sounded naive even inside her own head, she cleared her throat. "Anyway," she told George brightly, "I'm glad I ran into you. You know Emily Williams, right?"

"Uh-huh." George looked a bit perplexed at the sudden change of topic.

Stevie plowed ahead. "Well, then you probably heard she's moving soon. We're having a good-bye party for her a week from Saturday at my house— it should be a blast. We want all her friends to come." She smiled. "You'll be there, won't you?"

"The Saturday after this one?" George asked. "Um, okay. Is—uh, is Callie going to be there?"

"Of course." Stevie was careful to keep her smile as cheerful as ever. "See you then, okay?"

As she hurried off toward Belle's stall, she tried to tell herself she'd done all she could to help George. *He probably just needed someone to listen to him,* she thought. *And at least now he'll have a whole week to look forward to seeing Callie at the party.* She bit her lower lip guiltily. *Whatever happens after that is up to him—and Callie.*

FIFTEEN

"This is kind of nice, isn't it?" Lisa commented, glancing around the Hansons' comfortable living room. "Sort of like old times."

"Nice?" Stevie shot her a disgruntled look. "Nice? You wouldn't be saying that if you were taking the PSATs in less than thirteen hours."

Carole smiled ruefully. "She probably would, actually," she said. "She wouldn't be worried because she'd know she was going to ace it."

"Very funny." Lisa couldn't help grinning sheepishly. It was true that it was easy to be relaxed and nostalgic when her PSATs and SATs were both behind her. She remembered how frantic she'd been while she was preparing for the important tests—not to mention how happy and relieved she'd been when her results had come weeks afterward and she'd found out that it had all paid off in excellent scores.

All that aside, she still thought it was awfully nice to be sitting there with her two best friends in the world, with the house to themselves and most of Friday evening still in front of them. Carole's father was out at some fancy political dinner in nearby Washington, D.C., but he had made sure the house was well stocked with pizza and junk food. "For once, I don't even miss Alex," Lisa commented contentedly.

Stevie snorted. "I never miss Alex." She was flipping through the pages in her PSAT study guide as she sprawled on the Hansons' couch. "I still can't believe my parents let him go to that soccer game at Chad's college tonight. I think the only reason they let me come over here is because they thought Lisa would be a good influence. And because I swore I'd be home—in bed—by ten-thirty." She glanced down at the page in front of her. "By the way, does anyone know what *bucolic* means?"

"I think it means something having to do with rural-type stuff," Carole volunteered, leaning forward from her seat in her father's favorite easy chair to reach for her soda glass. "You know, like sheep or pastures or whatever." She glanced at her watch, almost spilling the soda in her lap in the process. "That reminds me, *Paradise Ranch* comes on in a little while."

"I know. I'm watching the time." Lisa had no intention of missing an episode of the television show she'd worked on all summer in California.

Stevie checked her own watch. "Hey, we ought to take a break before it starts and call a few more people about the party."

Lisa nodded. They had all been spreading the word about Emily's farewell blowout since the day before, and they planned to call and invite as many people as they could that evening in between watching TV and reviewing PSAT vocabulary words. "Who wants to hit the phones next?"

"I will," Stevie volunteered, sitting up and pushing her book aside. "But only if you'll let me call Veronica and disinvite her."

Lisa and Carole exchanged a glance and a grin. None of them was happy that Veronica had heard about the party and invited herself via Scott, but the wealthy, self-centered girl had always irritated Stevie more than anyone. "Why don't you call A.J. first?" Lisa suggested. "I know he's not speaking to Phil these days, but we still ought to invite him."

"I guess," Stevie agreed reluctantly. She sighed as she walked toward the phone on Colonel Hanson's big mahogany desk. "I don't know what good it'll do, though. There's no way he'll come. He's not exactly a party kind of guy these days, in case you didn't notice."

"Call him," Lisa said firmly. She knew it was probably an exercise in futility, but she couldn't help hoping that A.J. would come. It would do him good to have some fun with his friends after his weeks of gloom and solitude. Besides, she was sure that if he and Phil spent a little time in the same room, A.J. would get over being angry.

Phil only did what he thought was best, Lisa thought as Stevie dialed the phone. *He was right to tell A.J.'s parents what was going on. How else could they help A.J. stop hurting?* It reminded her a little of her fight with Carole. Some secrets were better not kept—they only ended up hurting people more by their existence. Phil had done the right thing by speaking up.

Then again, there were secrets that might be better kept forever—like the secret between her and Alex. What would either of them gain if she told him she'd almost stayed in California? It wouldn't change the fact that she'd decided to come home instead. It wouldn't change the fact that she would have kept loving him either way. All it would do was open up wounds that had almost healed, cause arguments that might never lead to a resolution.

Maybe it would be better if I never told him, Lisa thought. *I don't want it to stand between us from now on. Besides, I may have to face this issue again soon enough when it's time to decide where I'm going to college. Why ruin the time we have together now?*

A month earlier it would have been unthinkable for her to consider keeping such an important secret from Alex. But just at the moment, it seemed even more unthinkable to risk their entire relationship by telling.

She glanced at Stevie, suddenly remembering that she and Alex weren't the only ones involved in this particular secret. Lisa had told her two best friends of her decision as soon as she'd made it. Carole seemed to have forgotten all about it, but Stevie had recently discovered that her twin still didn't know and begged Lisa to tell him. Lisa knew it would be unfair of her to ask Stevie to keep secrets from her own brother.

She didn't know what to do. All she knew was that she'd better decide soon, before too much more time had passed. It would be difficult enough to explain to Alex as it was, assuming she did decide to tell. . . .

Stevie hung up the phone, still hardly daring to believe what she'd just heard. "Amazing," she declared. "He said yes!"

Carole looked up from her study guide in surprise. "Really?"

Stevie nodded, a slow smile spreading across her face. People were really incredible sometimes. Just when you thought you had them figured out, they changed yet again. "He actually sounded pretty chipper," she said. "He's still mad at Phil—he made that clear enough—but otherwise he seemed almost normal."

"Maybe talking to his parents about this helped, then," Lisa said. "I read that it sometimes makes adoptees feel better if they can really believe that they were *chosen* by their new families, instead of thinking of themselves as having been given away by their birth families."

Stevie shrugged. She wasn't that interested in Lisa's little research project on the psychology of adoption issues. She was just glad that A.J. was sounding better, and that he'd promised to come to the party. "He said he was in the mood to let loose," she mused aloud. "That sounds like progress to me."

She returned to her seat on the couch, feeling optimistic. *Things are definitely on an upswing these days*, she thought, glancing down at her vocabulary list. A word jumped off the page at her.

"Karma," she said. "It's karma."

"I know that one," Carole said eagerly. "Wait, don't tell me. It's sort of like fate, right? It means that the stuff you do to other people reflects back on you and affects your own life."

Lisa nodded. "Actually I think it has to do with Buddhism," she said. "If you're nice to people in this life, Buddhists believe you'll be a better person in your next life. Or something like that."

Stevie shrugged. She hoped Phil wouldn't have to wait for his next life to reap the benefits of his good deed. Maybe if he and A.J. got a chance to talk at the party, work things out over a sweet cup of cider . . .

That reminded her that she had barely started thinking about refreshments. Making a mental note to discuss appropriate food and drink with Alex, she realized it was almost time for *Paradise Ranch* to start and she'd forgotten to call anyone besides A.J. Her conversation with him had wiped everything else out of her mind for a moment.

"I'll call more people at the first commercial break," she said, reaching for the remote control. There was going to be a lot to do if she wanted to make Emily's party a success. But she was sure she could do it with a little help from her friends—and some creative thinking. It had already occurred to her that the party would be a perfect opportunity for Scott to get in some extra campaigning for the election. Her mind was overflowing with ideas for him to get his ideas across. . . . She smiled as she thought about all her plans, looking forward to the coming days and weeks.

Carole forced herself to put her study guide down and settle back in her chair as the familiar opening credits of *Paradise Ranch* appeared on the television screen. She'd spent every spare moment cramming for tomorrow morning's test—in between taking care of business at Pine Hollow, preparing for the Colesford Horse Show, and trying to keep up with her regular homework. It was hard to believe that the week had passed so quickly.

At least after tomorrow it will be over, she thought nervously. *I just hope I can pull it off. I've got to pull it off.*

Glancing at her study guide again, she gulped. She had studied hard and was pretty sure she was adequately prepared, but the memory of that failed history test haunted her. That and the memory of what she'd done to pass the makeup test . . .

I can't ever let that happen again, she told herself firmly, hardly aware of the tiny figures moving about on the TV in front of her, though her eyes were locked on the screen. *It was a mistake, and I've got to put it behind me. Nobody ever has to know. I've learned my lesson.*

She did her best to put that out of her mind and focus on the show. Onscreen, one character was arguing with another about something or other that Carole couldn't quite figure out. It reminded her a bit of her fight with Ben the week before. She wasn't quite sure what that had all been about, either. Why had he suddenly decided to pry into her life? It wasn't like him.

It seems like hardly anybody is acting like themselves these days, she thought with a little sigh. *A.J.*

has turned from a nice guy to an ogre and back again so many times now that my head is spinning. Lisa sure wasn't acting like her calm, rational self when she got so mad at me about the Prancer secret. Self-centered Veronica diAngelo shows up to help A.J. and actually gets through to him. And now Ben decides to change into Mr. Busybody. . . .

Still, no matter how the people in her life changed, Carole could always count on the horses to be their own wonderful, honest selves. At that thought, Samson immediately sprang into her mind. She'd only had time for a brief session with him that afternoon, but it had gone very well. At the rate he was improving, she was starting to think that by the time the Colesford show came along he would be positively peerless even in that rarefied competition.

I can't wait, she thought dreamily. *It's going to be so much fun to be there with him. Even if he stumbles or something and we don't get the blue, just having the chance to ride such an incredible horse in such an incredible show will be reward enough in itself. Win or lose, it's certain to be one of the most memorable days of my entire life!*

"Ready to go?" Alex asked with a yawn the next morning.

"Ready as I'll ever be." Stevie shoved Bear's nose out of her cornflakes and carried the nearly empty bowl to the sink. Alex's yawn was catching, and she yawned, too. "I'll drive if you want. Don't forget, we promised to pick up Carole on the way."

It was so early that Mr. and Mrs. Lake were still in bed. But Stevie and Alex had been in the kitchen for almost half an hour, eating breakfast and quizzing each other on mathematical formulas.

As Stevie sleepily pulled on her jacket, she heard footsteps on the stairs. A moment later Michael entered the kitchen, still in his pajamas, his hair tousled.

"Hi, Michael," Stevie said. "Do you know where my camera is?"

"Why?" Michael asked suspiciously, squinting at her beneath sleepy eyelids.

Stevie opened her mouth to answer. *I want to get a picture of you looking all cute and sleepy and rumpled like a baby fawn.* That was what she'd planned to say, but the words wouldn't come out. Suddenly all she could think about was George Wheeler—how awkward and vulnerable he had been the other night in the stable as he'd revealed his feelings for Callie.

Suddenly Michael reminded her of George— and of herself, a little, back when she was just getting to know Phil. No matter how different people seemed on the outside, the tender feelings of new, first, uncertain love were just as easy to bruise in one as in another. Stevie had fought back against her brothers' teasing back then, had never let them see how much their jokes and obnoxious comments really bothered her. But for some reason, being teased about her relationship with Phil had hurt a lot more than all the other teasing rolled up together. It had been the one area in which even she had felt uncertain and vulnerable, just the way George obviously felt about his crush on Callie, and just the way Michael probably felt about his relationship with Fawn.

We were all pretty young back then, she thought. *They didn't know any better when they teased me about Phil. But I should know better now. I should know that other people have feelings that can get hurt if I don't pay attention to how I treat them.* How could she expect to help A.J., to be there for any of her friends, if she couldn't remember that?

"I—uh, I just wanted to make sure I had enough film," she stammered lamely, realizing that her brothers were still waiting for a response. "Um, before the party next week. I want to get plenty of pictures of Emily before she leaves."

Alex cocked a skeptical eyebrow at her. Michael frowned as though wondering if he was missing

214

some sort of obscure joke. Stevie just smiled innocently at both of them, enjoying their surprise.

"By the way, Michael," she said casually. "I'm, uh, sorry if I've been on your case this week. Fawn's a really nice person, and I'm glad you two are happy together."

Michael's jaw dropped. He stared at her, speechless.

Stevie smiled. She didn't know if her apology would make any real difference in her brother's life, but to her amazement it immediately made her feel like a better person. *I guess that's what karma is really all about,* she thought, remembering the vocabulary word from the evening before. Suddenly she was wide awake, alert, and brimming with confidence, ready to give the PSATs her very best shot.

"Come on," she told Alex cheerfully. "We don't want to be late."

She found herself whistling as she headed out the door toward the car. Out of the corner of her eye, she caught Alex shooting her perplexed little glances.

She didn't really blame him for being surprised. *Sometimes,* she thought contentedly, *I even surprise myself!*

ABOUT THE AUTHOR

BONNIE BRYANT is the author of more than a hundred books about horses, including The Saddle Club series, Saddle Club Super Editions, and the Pony Tails series. She has also written novels and movie novelizations under her married name, B. B. Hiller.

Ms. Bryant began writing The Saddle Club in 1986. Although she had done some riding before that, she intensified her studies then and found herself learning right along with her characters Stevie, Carole, and Lisa. She claims that they are all much better riders than she is.

Ms. Bryant was born and raised in New York City. She still lives there, in Greenwich Village, with her two sons.

You'll always remember your first love.

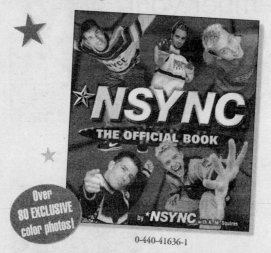